# "What's your span?" he asked briskly

"Ten keys." She spread her fingers as wide as possible across his palm to demonstrate, and suddenly, without any warning at all, something happened.

Her fingertips felt as though they were on fire, drawing lines of heat across his sensitive palms, and apparently he felt it, too, because his eyes jerked up in surprise at the same time hers did, and he drew in a quick, audible breath.

Madeline froze, transfixed by both the astounding signals racing from her hands to her brain, and the hypnotic quality of his gaze. Even as she watched, his pupils expanded until a circle of hot black nearly obliterated the green, and for some reason that frightened her.

"I don't think I ever really heard my music until I heard you play it today," he said, but somehow his tone sounded more like a threat than an accolade. "I'm not about to let anything interfere with that."

**MELINDA CROSS** would love her readers to believe she was kidnapped as a child by an obscure nomadic tribe and rescued by a dashing adventurer. Actually, though, she is a wonderfully imaginative American writer who is married to a true romantic. Every spring, without fail, when the apple orchard blooms, her husband gathers a blanket, glasses and wine and leads Melinda out to enjoy the fragrant night air. Romantic fantasy? Nonsense, she says. This is the stuff of real life.

## Books by Melinda Cross

### HARLEQUIN PRESENTS

Don't miss any of our special offers. Write to us at the following address for information on our newest releases.

Harlequin Reader Service
P.O. Box 1397, Buffalo, NY 14240
Canadian address: P.O. Box 603,
Fort Erie, Ont. L2A 5X3

# MELINDA CROSS

## *Heartsong*

# *Harlequin Books*

TORONTO • NEW YORK • LONDON
AMSTERDAM • PARIS • SYDNEY • HAMBURG
STOCKHOLM • ATHENS • TOKYO • MILAN
MADRID • WARSAW • BUDAPEST • AUCKLAND

Harlequin Presents first edition November 1992
ISBN 0-373-11504-0

Original hardcover edition published in 1991
by Mills & Boon Limited

HEARTSONG

Printed in U.S.A.

# CHAPTER ONE

MADELINE sat in the deep shadows towards the back of the great auditorium, her chin lifted slightly, her eyes closed. A pale, almost white curve of hair stirred against her chin as she breathed, but save for that, and the barely perceptible movement of her fingers in her lap, she was perfectly motionless.

Her complexion was every bit as pale as her hair, a phenomenon that prompted disbelieving double-takes whenever she left her Manhattan apartment. Normally this unkind attention of strangers made it far more pleasant to stay home, but today was special; today she hadn't even minded the rude stares of people on the street; had hardly noticed them, in fact.

At the moment there was a serenity to her features that seemed out of place in the concert hall, where almost every other face was tight with stress. Madeline looked around at the other contestants scattered among the hundreds of empty seats. She guessed that most were concert pianists, out of their element in a competition where they would not be allowed to play classical music. She'd overheard a few of them complaining in the seats nearby.

'What the hell does a popular composer like

Elias Shepherd want with a classical pianist anyway?' one young man had grumbled.

'Who cares?' his companion had answered. 'As long as he's got the money to hand out prizes like this, I'll play anything he wants to hear. The trouble is, I'm not sure I can play his kind of music.'

Madeline could see the nearly palpable tension in their faces—could almost *smell* it beneath the covering fragrances of their colognes—and in a very distant, almost absent way she felt sorry for them all. Theirs was an uncertainty that came from the desperate need to please others, and Madeline had long since given up trying to do that. She wasn't here for anyone's approval; she was here for the prize money, period. Even the amount promised to the tenth-place finalist seemed like a fortune; the possibility of placing higher had never even occurred to her. She wasn't a performer, after all, only a New York City piano teacher trying to make ends meet, and optimism was a condition she had shed with her childhood.

The memories of that childhood had been shelved long ago, much as old, useless papers were crowded into a box and jammed to the back of a cupboard. But occasionally, at times like these when she was forced to idleness, those memories came creeping to the forefront of her thoughts, like a stain in the carpet that reappeared time and again, no matter how thoroughly it was scrubbed away.

Illegitimate. The word stood out in her mind, more like a comment on her existence itself than on the circumstances of her birth. Father unknown, mother a desperate teenager barely out of childhood herself—Madeline had entered the world unwanted and unexpected, shattering young lives even before she took her first breath.

Years later she learned that the adoption service had given her yet another label, and the new one was even worse: 'difficult to place'. She never knew what had earned her that title, but suspected that, even as a baby, her odd, colourless appearance had been a deterrent to young couples who dreamed of rosy-cheeked, roly-poly babies with bright blue eyes and rosebud mouths.

Whatever the reason, her childhood had been peppered with the memories of a succession of foster homes—good places, for the most part, and with good, decent people—but they'd slipped in and out of her life like sand running through her fingers. Madeline the child had learned early that no bond was permanent; no affection, however sincere, was lasting; and Madeline the young woman had no reason to believe otherwise. The only ongoing relationship she had ever experienced was with an inanimate object—the piano—and, although most would have considered that a tragic admission of an empty life, Madeline had never had more than that, and so it was enough.

Her first foster mother had propped her on a

piano bench when she was still a toddler, and had been promptly rewarded with an awe-struck, strangely pathetic smile from her solemn little charge. The white things that had looked to a child like monstrous teeth made wondrous, magical sounds, and Madeline had fallen in love.

The circumstances of her life had allowed for only a few formal lessons, but those had been enough. Armed with the most basic instruction, Madeline had taught herself to play the masters—Bach, Beethoven, Chopin, Mozart—and now, at twenty-five, she was skilled enough to make a tentative living teaching other children what she had had to learn on her own. The irony of that pleased her sense of order, and she was basically content—or at least she had been, until a couple of years ago. That was when she had started to play the music of Elias Shepherd, and, almost instantly, she had fallen in love for the second time in her life.

Elias Shepherd. The mere thought of his name brought her sharply aware, and she opened large grey eyes that called to mind nothing so much as an arctic wilderness. She glanced towards the brightly lit stage far in front of her, and saw that a worker was opening the concert grand, adjusting the music stand, testing the microphone at the podium at stage right.

It would begin soon. The first Annual Elias Shepherd Piano Competition would start any minute, and for this one afternoon, at least, the aduitorium would ring with his music.

*Her* music, she corrected herself, because that was the way she had come to think of his recent work, so sharply different from the light show tunes, the movie scores and the popular music that had made him famous. Suddenly, two years ago, the nature of his music had changed, become darker somehow. She felt the echo of her own despair in his new haunting, poignant melodies; heard the thrum of her own loneliness in the pounding of the bass; it was almost as if he spoke for her through his music; almost as if she spoke for him when she played it. Unfortunately, the world didn't agree with her. The critics panned his new work unmercifully, the movie and television producers had stopped hiring him to create their musical scores, and the audiences no longer flocked to his concerts.

'Jonathan Parks?' The call came from the stage, and the house lights dimmed even further as a contestant rose from his seat in the middle of the auditorium and walked stiffly down the aisle.

Madeline squirmed a little in her seat and grabbed the armrests, her features composed, but her eyes alight with anticipation.

Jonathan Parks was a tall, thin-faced man with longish blond hair and sharp features—the classic picture of the aspiring concert pianist as he settled at the piano, his head thrown back, his long fingers poised over the keys.

Madeline closed her eyes at the first chord, prepared to be transported by the desolate beauty of one of Shepherd's compositions, but after a few bars her eyes opened and she frowned. As skilled as he obviously was, Parks was playing the piece he'd chosen all wrong. He was muddling the timing, inserting cloying sentimentality that simply didn't belong in the crisp, brutally simple phrasing.

Eventually Parks finished, was followed by another competitor, then another, and another, and soon Madeline ceased to hear the music coming from the stage and only heard the music in her head, the way she would have played it.

Finally, hours later, her own call came. 'Madeline Chambers?' The acoustic properties of the concert hall absorbed her name and flattened it.

'I'm here.' She rose slowly, stiff from sitting so long. She was almost the very last contestant, and noticed as she approached the stage that the auditorium was nearly empty.

'Are you ready, Miss Chambers?' came a voice from beyond the glare of footlights as soon as she was settled at the piano. It was a gentle, feminine voice, chosen to soothe the frazzled nerves of stressed competitors.

'Yes.' Madeline nodded, smiling almost reverently at the pristine keyboard before her, so unlike the chipped, yellowing keys of her own ancient grand at home.

This is for you, Mr Shepherd, she thought

silently. Whether you know it or not, this is the way your music should sound.

And then her fingers touched the keys in a loving caress, lifted to position, and the soul of a man she had never met came to life beneath her hands.

In tenth row centre, a man's face stilled suddenly, and deep green eyes focused on the stage.

Two hours later Madeline was back in her tiny, one-bedroom apartment, happily trading her low heels and black dress for slippers and a fuzzy white robe. She scrubbed the make-up from her face, then stood before the mirror in her bedroom, brushing her hair until it fluffed in a pale, crackling halo around her shoulders.

She paused in mid-stroke, her eyes narrowed critically at the dark, lush circle of lashes that surrounded what looked like icy grey stones. It wasn't bad enough that her hair and eyes and complexion were all so light that they sometimes seemed transparent; added to that were incongruously dark lashes that looked like somebody else's body parts, slapped on her by mistake at the last minute. If she'd been at all concerned with her physical appearance, she could have faulted herself endlessly—aside from the regrettable lack of colouring, her mouth was too wide, her lips too full, her body too tall and slender—but the eyelashes were easily the most offensive feature she had, simply because they didn't match the rest of her.

She sighed and turned away from the mirror, relieved to be shuttered once again in her apartment, away from the stares of strangers.

She was halfway through the jumble of living-room furniture on her way to the kitchen when a hard knock sounded at her door, making her frown.

She tightened the belt on her robe, walked to the door, cracked it reluctantly and peeked around the edge.

'Congratulations.'

Madeline's eyes lifted slowly upward until they focused on the shadowed features of a man she'd never seen before. 'I beg your pardon?' she said, squinting into the dim light of the hallway.

'I said congratulations. This belongs to you.'

He was holding a rectangle of white towards her, but she barely noticed. A tip of his head had brought his eyes into the light, and Madeline stared at them, fascinated. They were the deep, luminescent green one would expect to find in a spring garden, but never in anyone's eyes.

He tolerated her silent stare for a moment, apparently amused by it, then inclined his head slightly. 'There's a cheque for a great deal of money in this envelope, Miss Chambers.'

Incredible eyes or not, a sales pitch was still a sales pitch. Madeline sighed and arched one light brow. 'Really? Well, that's a very novel opening line, but I'm not interested in buying anything, thank you.'

He chuckled just as she moved to close the door. 'It's the prize money for the piano competition, Miss Chambers. You won.'

Her breathing stopped, and her eyes narrowed suspiciously. 'That's not possible. I was told we'd be notified by mail.'

'Everyone else will be notified by mail. The winner should get a special delivery, don't you think?'

The winner. Madeline felt herself sag a little against the door as she tried to absorb the news, tried to remember just how much money had been promised for first place. 'I won?' she whispered, hating the uncertain quaver in her voice, but unable to control it just this once. 'Are you sure?'

'Yes. I'm absolutely sure.'

She nodded slowly, her thoughts numb. She had had such modest dreams, never entertaining the notion that Elias Shepherd would select her as the winner, let alone send someone over with the prize money that very night.

Someone you're letting stand out of the draughty hallway, she realised suddenly, and jerked the door wide. 'Please, come in,' she said, gesturing towards a cluster of couch and chairs jammed into one corner of the living-room, dwarfed by the ancient baby grand piano she had saved for years to buy. 'Sit down, if you like. I was just about to make some Irish coffee. . .'

The words caught in her throat when he turned to face her and she saw him in full light for the first time. Instantly, even though she had never met him, never seen his photograph, she knew he was Elias Shepherd. Whatever it was that pulled at her from his music was also there in his face, and the immediate sense of recognition stunned her. She'd been in love with the intellect and the spirit that created Elias Shepherd's music for almost two years, but she had never really considered that that spirit would be visible on a man's face.

'You're Elias Shephered,' she murmured, afraid to move, afraid even to blink, for fear the vision would dissolve.

He stared right back at her for what seemed like a long time, then nodded.

Unconsciously she straightened, and, absurd as it was, even in housecoat and slippers there was an almost regal air about her, as if her body knew instinctively that this was the only proper way to stand before this particular man.

I know you, she thought numbly. I've known you for a long time.

He looked every bit as dark and haunted as his music, with black brows jetting over those startling green eyes and a grimly set mouth slashed across a square jaw. But there was something else beneath all the sombre intensity—something clean and bright and hard that made her think of the pinwheeling brilliance of sunlight on the ocean.

It startled her when he spoke, and she wondered how long she had been standing there, staring at him in silence. 'The coffee sounds wonderful. Thank you.'

'You're welcome,' she replied tonelessly, but she remained motionless, unable to tear her eyes away. Finally she forced herself to turn and retreat towards the kitchen.

Irish coffee was easy—she'd made it a hundred times before in her life—but tonight the process seemed endlessly complicated; very nearly beyond her capabilities.

When she returned to the living-room she found him sitting stiffly on the couch, watching her approach with a kind of mystified wariness. Their fingers touched briefly as he took the mug from her hand, and Madeline sank into the chair that faced the couch, confused by the heat his touch had generated.

They both sipped from their mugs, then he said, 'Your performance today moved me.'

Her head jerked up at the dark, rolling sound of his voice. She avoided his eyes, concentrating instead on the way his black hair swept backwards over his ears and curled at the collar of his shirt. It was a white shirt, she noticed for the first time; unbuttoned at the neck as if he'd just jerked off a tie and tossed it aside.

'You've never competed before, have you?'

'No.' She started shaking her head, then had to remind herself to stop. 'Was it so obvious?'

'Certainly not.' His mouth moved as if it wanted to smile. 'It's just that I attend almost every competition. I would have remembered a pianist like you.'

Madeline took another drink and felt the whiskey warm her throat. 'I'm not a pianist at all, really. Just a piano teacher.'

This time he did smile, briefly. 'And Shakespeare was just a writer.'

Her eyes barely had time to widen at the outrageous comparison before he shocked her again.

'I'd like to hire you, Miss Chambers. I want you to work with me full-time on a very important project; playing my music; maybe recording it, eventually.'

Her hesitation was only as long as a heartbeat. 'All right.'

The mug stopped halfway to his mouth. 'All right?' he repeated, the green eyes seeming to darken as she watched. 'That's all there is to it?'

Madeline frowned uncertainly as her tongue darted to moisten her lower lip, wondering why her reply had surprised him.

'Don't you want to know about the salary? The working conditions? *Anything?*'

She shook her head mindlessly. 'You're Elias Shepherd,' she told him for the second time that evening, as if that explained everything.

He regarded her quietly for a moment. 'What do you know about me?'

'Everything,' she whispered, then frowned, realising how foolish that sounded. 'Nothing,' she added, confused.

'So which is it?'

She looked down into her mug, pale brows furrowed, lips pressed together in consternation. What *did* she know about Elias Shepherd? She was barely familiar with the music that had made him famous: the show tunes, the popular songs, the movie scores he'd written over the past ten years—none of that had touched her. 'I just know the music you've written over the past two years. That's all.'

'That's everything,' he said quietly, and she felt something deep and profound click into place at the very centre of her being.

'All right, then,' she heard him say after a moment. 'These are the ground rules. We'll work at Rosewood, my place in the country. We won't be disturbed there.' A smile tried to find the corners of her mouth. 'You'll have to leave your home, give up your students, your friends, your family, your social life—your life itself, really—for as long as the job lasts.'

She nodded silently, still looking down into her mug, wondering how she was going to contain all this joy; how she was going to remain sitting here affecting calm when she wanted to leap and shout and——

'The hours will be terrible, I'm impatient and

irritable and impossible to work with. . .'
Madeline risked a glance upwards at his harsh
tone. 'As a matter of fact, the only decent thing
about this job will be the salary. That, I can
promise you, will be excellent.'

Madeline focused on a jagged crack in the
plaster wall behind him, smiling a little because
he thought things like hours and conditions and
salary were important. How could she tell him?
How could she explain that his music had been
the single spot of brightness in an otherwise
drab existence; that, in some mystical way she
couldn't articulate, she had belonged to him
since she'd started playing his music? Leaving
her life to follow him now was just the physical
completion of a spiritual commitment she'd
made a long time ago.

'You've offered me a job,' she finally said
quietly, commanding his eyes, 'and I've
accepted. Are you retracting the offer?'

He searched her face carefully, as if he was
looking for a sign of weakness. 'No,' he said
finally. 'I'm not that gallant. The offer stands.'

'Good.' She nodded firmly, and for some
reason her certainty seemed to frustrate him.

'This won't be a lark, Miss Chambers,' he
warned her, green eyes narrowing slightly. 'My
music is the only thing that matters to me. I
don't have the time or the inclination to tiptoe
over people's feelings. As a matter of fact, I
don't have much patience for dealing with

people at all. Working with me is a very lonely proposition.'

Madeline looked at him quietly, trying not to smile. 'All right, Mr Shepherd. You win. I'll pay *you* for the job. How much do you want?'

Without warning he laughed out loud, and the sound was so discordant, so unpractised, that Madeline wondered if he'd ever laughed before at all. 'All right, Miss Chambers,' he said, a smile still playing at the corners of his mouth. 'Organise your affairs; arrange to leave the city for a while. . .'

'For how long?'

'It depends on a lot of things. It could be for a month. . .' he hesitated for a moment, searching her face with the strangest expression '. . .or it could be for much longer.'

She looked at him without saying anything and his brow twitched at something he saw in her face. Green eyes met grey ones and held them for a prolonged moment.

'I think we'll work well together, Miss Chambers.' He leaned forward and reached across the narrow distance between the couch and chair, taking one of her hands in his, turning it over in his palm, staring at it with wonder as it it were an object of great value. His touch was completely impersonal—he was simply examining the tool that would implement his music—and, perhaps because of that, Madeline didn't flinch as she normally did when someone made physical contact. 'Give me your other hand,' he commanded without looking up, scooting even farther forward on the couch until their knees almost brushed.

She put her mug on a nearby table and obediently offered her other hand. He held them both in his palms, spreading his fingers beneath to make her spread hers. It was a little like being examined by a doctor, and she watched absently, strangely removed from that part of her body he touched.

'What's your span?' he asked briskly.

'Ten keys.' She spread her fingers as wide as possible across his palm to demonstrate, and suddenly, without any warning at all, something happened.

Her fingertips felt as though they were on fire, drawing lines of heat across his sensitive palms, and apparently he felt it too, because his eyes jerked up in surprise at the same time hers did, and he drew in a quick, audible breath.

Madeline froze, transfixed by both the astounding signals racing from her hands to her brain, and the hypnotic quality of his gaze. Even as she watched, his pupils expanded until a circle of hot black nearly obliterated the green, and for some reason that frightened her.

She jerked her hands from his in a panic, her own eyes wide and startled.

For a long time their eyes remained locked in a gaze neither seemed able to break, and then at last he closed his eyes, turned his head away, and lifted his shoulders in a shrug that said nothing had happened here, and if it had, it was hardly worth noting.

'Be ready at ten tomorrow morning,' he said gruffly, rising to his feet, crossing to the door almost before she was aware he had moved at all. 'I'll show you Rosewood, and we'll work out the details.'

At the last moment, just as he was about to step out into the hallway, he turned around and looked straight at her, still sitting in the chair where he'd left her. His expression was dark and forbidding, and seemed to accuse her of some terrible affront.

'I don't think I ever really heard my music until I heard you play it today,' he said, but somehow his tone sounded more like a threat than an accolade. 'I'm not about to let anything interfere with that.'

For a long time after he had left, Madeline sat motionless in her chair, staring at her hands.

# CHAPTER TWO

MADELINE awoke the next morning to an almost painful heightening of her senses. She winced at the piercing sounds of traffic in the street below; she squinted at the strangely bright morning light coming through the window; even her lightweight blanket seemed unbearably heavy on her body. She started to fling it off, then stopped, frowning as she lay in bed, trying to remember when she'd felt like this before; trying to catch the elusive memory flitting through her brain, running from one hiding place to another.

It had been a long time ago—she knew that— but she couldn't remember when. It was the kind of extraordinary expectation a child might feel on Christmas morning, but it hadn't been a Christmas. Whenever it was, it had been bigger than that; even more promising.

She frowned hard, trying to remember, then finally surrendered to forgetfulness. Past anticipations weren't important now anyway. She was going to work with Elias Shepherd: play his music, live in his house, actually witness the miracle of his musical creation; anticipating that was about all she could handle.

Dressing in black hadn't been intentional, but

she nodded with approval when she examined her reflection after dressing. This was a pivotal day in her life, after all, and that her appearance reflected the solemnity of the occasion seemed fitting.

She wore black boots, slim black jeans, and a high-necked black sweater in deference to the chill of early spring. She'd never been to a country home, but she imagined that this was what one should wear to tramp the inevitably muddy roads and brambly fields she'd seen in pictures and read about. Only her hair spoiled the sedate image. Refusing to stay neatly pinned in a dignified bun, it rioted over her shoulders in a flurry of bright, wispy static, looking ridiculously frivolous. Still, it was only a minor irritation. As she always did, Madeline forgot all about her appearance the moment she turned away from the mirror.

At precisely ten o'clock she opened the door to Shepherd's firm knock, and smiled uncertainly. He looked totally different from the way he had the night before; softer, she thought, for want of a better word.

He wore a light raincoat over a sweater of deep rose—angora, maybe, or lambswool, or one of the other precious knits that made you want to run your hands over them—and the colour warmed his face and made her think that perhaps he wasn't quite as grim as he had seemed last night. Even his black hair seemed boyish, tossed by a playful spring wind into a

soft wave over his forehead, curling over his
ears in a mockery of last night's swept-back,
slick sophistication.

'You look different,' she said matter-of-factly.

'So do you. I like you in black.' It was a
personal remark, and she hadn't been prepared
for it. Nor was she prepared for the intensity of
his gaze or its effect on her. It was too much like
that strange moment last night, that moment
she'd convinced herself had never really happened, when the connection between them had
plummeted from the security of the spiritual to
the dangerous, unfamiliar territory of the physical. Perhaps that was why she reacted so
strongly when he extended his hand palm-up
and said, 'Shall we go?'

It was such an innocent question, such a
harmless one, and yet instantly she felt a stab of
that old childhood feeling—a feeling she had
hoped she would never feel again, because it
was only a precursor to disappointment.

She stared miserably at his outstretched hand,
remembering all the other outstretched hands
that belonged to the Andersons, or the Stuarts,
or the Kruegers, or the Millers, or any of the
other temporary parents who had led her away
to temporary homes. 'Shall we go, Madeline?'
they had all asked, taking her little hand and
filling her young heart with hope that theirs
would be the home that would last, the love
that would last, but it never was, because
nothing lasted forever.

'Madeline?' He was watching her face carefully, his brow furrowed, and why not? She was acting like an idiot. 'Is there something wrong? Have you changed your mind?'

She took a deep breath, forced a small smile, and slipped her fingers into the cup of his large palm. 'No,' she said quietly. 'I haven't changed my mind.'

He tipped his head and studied her for a moment. 'Are you sure you're ready?'

'I'm ready,' she said firmly, wondering if that was really the most important question she'd ever been asked in her life, or if it only seemed that way.

He drove them in silence to an address in the East Seventies, a fashionable neighbourhood of restored brownstones and brick pavements that seemed further removed from the frantic bustle of downtown Manhattan than the actual distance that separated it.

'First stop,' he said as he helped her from the car. 'There's someone I want you to meet before we head up to Rosewood.'

A gust of wind played with his hair, giving him the illusion of carefree youth as they mounted the concrete steps, but it was only an illusion. There was nothing carefree about the set of his features as he rapped the brass knocker on the brownstone's door; nothing youthful in the green eyes that appraised her silently as they waited on the step.

It was only a man who opened the door—a

man like a thousand other men, Madeline thought—and yet she had the feeling that the door had opened on a panoramic view of sunrise, a light almost too bright to look at.

The man's eyes fastened on hers with a forthright stare that made her blush, although she couldn't have said why. 'Hello, Elias,' he murmured, without once taking his eyes from Madeline.

Elias mumbled something in reply, but Madeline's gaze was fixed on the man in the doorway. Everything about him was disarming—the careless tumble of rich brown curls over dark, merry eyes; an effortless smile that seemed to say smiling was what lips were for. In spite of her discomfort, Madeline found herself returning his smile, helpless to do otherwise, liking him before he spoke another word.

He startled her by grasping both her hands and squeezing them lightly. 'So you're magic Madeline. My God, Elias. Angel hair and fairy dust. She's spectacular!'

She didn't know whether to smile or frown at the outlandish comment.

'Don't be ridiculous, David,' Elias said brusquely, pushing his way past him into the foyer. 'She's a pianist, not a pin-up, and the magic I told you about is in her hands. Take a look at them. She's got an amazing span.'

Her hands still firmly locked in his, Madeline smiled hesitantly as he pulled her gently inside, kicking the door closed behind her.

'Honest to God, Elias,' David blustered in exasperation, shaking Madeline's hands in his for emphasis, 'sometimes I'm absolutely convinced that you've been dead for years and just forgot to lie down. A woman like this, and you want me to look at her *hands*?'

Madeline blinked up at him, astounded by the things he was saying. She was as numbly pliable as a rag-doll when he tucked her hand possessively in the crook of his elbow and led her into an elegantly furnished living-room where two love-seats faced each other in front of a crackling fire. The low table between them held a coffee service and a silver tray of Danish pastries. David pulled her down next to him on one of the love-seats, and, although close physical contact normally made her nervous, she felt surprisingly comfortable next to this particular man.

'Madeline Chambers, this is David Whitney, my manager,' Elias made the perfunctory introduction as he sat opposite them.

'And the warm, friendly half of this partnership,' David added. 'Sort of the balance for the black-hearted genius, if you know what I mean.'

Elias scowled at him. 'Tell her about the project, David. That's why I brought her here.' He poured himself a cup of coffee and stood abruptly. 'I have some calls to make before we leave for Rosewood.'

David watched him leave the room, his seemingly perpetual smile a little tentative, then he busied himself with the coffee. He passed Madeline a cup, turning sideways to appraise her with a curious smile. 'My God,' he said with a little shake of his head. 'And you can play the piano, too?'

Madeline frowned at him over her cup, baffled, and for some reason that made David laugh.

'Oh, brother. You're one in a million, aren't you? I feel like I'm watching a lamb walk off with a rabid wolf. Working with Elias isn't going to be easy, you know.'

'So he tells me.'

'And he's telling you the truth. He's been a virtual recluse for the past couple of years, and if he ever did know how to relate to people he's forgotten by now. There's only one thing in life he cares about, and that's his music.'

'I know that.'

David frowned, shifting his position uncomfortably. 'The thing is, it seems a little strange, your agreeing to go off to work with him so readily. . . You're not in love with him, or anything stupid like that, are you?'

Her eyes flew wide and she nearly choked on her coffee. 'Good lord, no. We just met. I just. . . I just. . .love his music, that's all.'

David looked at her steadily. 'Elias *is* his music.'

She pressed her lips together nervously, not knowing what to say to that.

He forced a smile, then changed the subject

abruptly. 'His career depends on this project, you know, and, in a way, on you.'

'On me?' Madeline whispered. 'What do you mean?'

David tossed back the rest of his coffee as if it were a shot of whiskey, then carefully replced the cup in its saucer. Madeline had the feeling he was weighing each word carefully before he spoke. 'There was a time when he couldn't write enough music to satisfy the demand, you know. Every band wanted to record an Elias Shepherd song, every producer wanted an Elias Shepherd soundtrack. . .' he sighed and his shoulders slumped '. . .and then two years ago it all changed. Trouble is, he doesn't understand why. He can't hear the difference between what he used to write—the music the world loved—and what he's writing now. He thought a classical pianist might be what the work needed. That's why he sponsored the contest.'

Madeline studied him thoughtfully, thinking how strange it was that she started to love his music when the world started to hate it. 'What happened two years ago?' she asked.

David looked at her for a moment. 'His marriage ended,' he said flatly.

The words gave Madeline pause, and she realised that she'd never thought of the creator of the music she loved as a mere mortal, with all the personal baggage that implied.

'I didn't know he'd been married,' she said quietly.

'He was. . .for a time. When the marriage ended, a lot of other things ended for Elias, too. His music changed; his life changed. . .' He shrugged away the rest of the thought and forced a smile that was just a little bit too bright. 'But that's all in the past, and we're supposed to be talking about the future.' He refilled their cups and turned on the love-seat to face her. 'You'll be working on a soundtrack for a movie. The producer is an old friend of Elias's, and the truth is, he's taking a hell of a risk giving Elias a contract at all, considering the public response to the music he's been writing lately. Everyone seems to hate it.'

Something in David's tone made her smile at him. 'But you don't, do you?'

David shrugged and looked away awkwardly. 'Sometimes. . .not often, but sometimes. . . I listen to the stuff he's writing now and I think he has the potential to be one of the really great ones, you know?' He looked back at her expectantly.

'I think he already is,' she said quietly.

His brows lifted slightly, giving him a solemn aspect, but it was short-lived. 'Well, from an agent's point of view, you've got to be marketable to be great.'

'That sounds pretty mercenary. What happened to "art for art's sake"?'

He shrugged off her disapproval. 'When art appeals to everyone, when it *touches* everyone, that's greatness, isn't it? And that's what Elias has lost in his music—that elusive something that touches people. No one denies that his work is technically masterful, but a lot of people think it has no heart, no feeling at all.'

Madeline smiled sadly. 'Then they aren't listening.'

David cocked his head, studying her, and for a moment Madeline had the feeling that he felt deeply sorry for her, although she couldn't imagine why.

The very air in the room seemed to part when Elias returned. He looked at David first, then Madeline. 'I called the studio and told them they'd have a sample tape in a month, which means we don't have a minute to waste, Madeline. Grab a Danish and we'll eat in the car on the way to Rosewood. We'll talk terms after you've seen the place. Coming, David?'

'Not this time.' David shook his head, looking at Madeline with a small, unreadable smile. When Elias turned his back and headed for the door, he pressed a business card into Madeline's hand. 'Call me when you need a friend,' he said simply.

# CHAPTER THREE

WHILE Elias was preoccupied with driving through the mild chaos of Sunday morning traffic, Madeline eyed him surreptitiously from the passenger seat of the luxury sedan. This is Elias Shepherd, she kept telling herself, possibly one of the greatest composers of this century, critics notwithstanding. You are sitting next to man destined to be a legend.

But for some reason she was having trouble thinking of him as a legend. He didn't look like a legend, sitting there behind the wheel, concentrating on the road ahead just like any other ordinary driver—he looked like a man, and Madeline found that very disconcerting.

'We may not be back until very late,' he warned her before they had gone two blocks.

'That's all right. I don't schedule students for the weekend.'

'No plans for the evening?'

She suppressed a smile. 'I've never had much time for a social life.' After a brief hesitation, she added, 'And I'm afraid I've never had much talent for it, either.'

Oddly enough, he smiled a little at that, and there was a comfortable silence between them as the car headed north and west on one of the

32

broad freeways that connected all the dots on a New York state map. Eventually the last grimy outposts of the city were lost behind them, and the land began a gentle undulation towards the rounded tops of ancient mountains, still too distant to see.

Madeline watched the landscape unroll outside her window, absently noticing the countryside embracing spring after a long, hard winter. Normally dignified Black Angus cattle cavorted like calves in newly opened pastures; creeks swollen with snowmelt tumbled in every gulley; and the green flutter of furled leaves made it look as though every tree was quivering in anticipation of its rebirth.

It should have been a magical, fairytale tapestry to someone whose world had always been limited to the concrete boundaries of the city, but to Madeline music had been the definition of beauty for so long that she'd almost forgotten how to appreciate anything else.

Over an hour later, Elias spoke the first words that had passed between them since they left the city. 'We're almost there,' he said as the car slowed on an exit ramp.

'Already?' Madeline blinked her way out of what seemed like a dream. She'd been staring at a spot on the dashboard for miles, playing one of his compositions in her mind.

She peered out of the side window at the narrow tar road they travelled along now, squinting at the bright splash of yellow daisies crowding right up to the asphalt on either side.

Elias glanced at her as the car topped a rise and coasted down into a village that looked more like a postcard than reality. 'Brighton Square,' he explained as the car slowed, its tyres thumping softly when the tar beneath them changed abruptly to old brick. 'My place is just a mile or so on the other side of town.'

Madeline nodded silently, her eyes busy. Quaint shop-fronts with colourful awnings lined the main street, wrought-iron lamp-posts called to mind another century, and a wildly gay tulip bed sprawled over the village green.

They probably invented the word 'charming' for places like this, Madeline thought, turning to watch through the back window as the tiny town receded into the distance. 'It's a lovely place,' she said. 'I can understand why you live here.'

'I live here because it's convenient,' he said, and there was a definite chill in his tone that made Madeline wonder what she had said wrong.

At last he turned the wheel sharply and entered a narrow drive banked with thick shrubs just beginning to leaf. 'This is it. Rosewood. You'll see the house in a minute.'

'I've never been in a house with a name before,' she said.

His jaw tightened momentarily, then relaxed. 'Don't get the wrong idea. It's no mansion. My

mother just had a passion for names, that's all.
She named almost everything she ever owned,
including this place, and the name stuck, even
after she died.'

'The house belonged to your parents?'

'Parent,' he corrected her, emphasising the
singular. 'They divorced shortly after I was born
and Mother never remarried.'

When the car rounded a turn in the drive that
brought them right up to the house, Madeline's
features went immediately slack, and without
realising it she leaned so close to the window
that her nose nearly pressed against the glass.
She would remember this moment later and be
grateful that her face had been turned away
from him, because she had felt the defensive
mask slipping; felt it being replaced by the
naked longing of the child she had once been,
and the pathetic wonder of that same child, to
see that sometimes fantasies came to life.

Home. Her lips formed that alien word in a
silent exhalation, fogging the glass as she gazed
out at the gingerbread jumble of red brick and
faded green shutters—it was the visualisation of
a dream she thought she'd forgotten; a dream
from those early, early years before life had
taught her not to dream at all.

Except for the ticking of the engine as it
cooled, there was complete silence in the car.
Elias studied Madeline as she stared out of the
window at the house, her profile softened and
somehow open, as if she was showing the house

a side of herself she never allowed people to
see. His black brows twitched in curiosity.

'I grew up in this house,' he said quietly.

Before she could stop herself, Madeline whispered, 'It's perfect.' The sound of her own voice
startled her, because she had never heard that
much emotion in it.

'It was once,' he said, staring out at the tangle
of unkempt shrubbery crowding the small front
porch. 'But that was a long time ago.' He sighed
and lifted his door-handle. 'Come on. I'll give
you the grand tour.'

Madeline thought that entering this particular
house as an adult was a little like getting up to
the ticket window right after the last seat had
been sold. You made it, all right; but it was just
too late. Maybe if she'd had a home like this as
a child, her life would have been different;
maybe the world wouldn't have been such a
cold, unforgiving school where all the lessons
were hard—but all the May bees died in June,
as one of her foster mothers had said.

Too late, too late, her thoughts repeated sadly
as she followed him through the house, her
expression frozen in a distant, polite smile.
Occasionally, unintentionally, her hand reached
out to trail across a papered wall; to touch a
porcelain doorknob a hundred years older than
she was; and in those brief seconds of physical
contact she thought of how perfect it all might
have been once, and how sad it was that it had
never been.

Most of the downstairs rooms were small, cosy, cluttered with comfortable old-fashioned furnishings and a lifetime of loving needle-work—his mother's, obviously—and suddenly she was intensely jealous of his boyhood; of the warmth and love any child would have felt growing up in a place like this, even without a father. It was the touch of a mother that Madeline felt in every room, almost like a living presence, welcoming her. . .

In an abrupt, angry gesture she shrugged away the fanciful notion, irritated with herself for even entertaining such a childishly mystical thought. She shut down her mind and concentrated on following Elias down a hallway that cut the house in half, running from the front entrance, past the staircase to the second floor, all the way back to an old-fashioned swinging door.

'The kitchen,' he announced unnecessarily as he stood aside to let her enter, first, but Madeline came to a sudden halt a few steps into the room. 'Anything wrong?' he asked from behind her.

Anything wrong? his words echoed in her mind. No. Of course not. Not unless there's something wrong with suddenly, inexplicably wanting to weep; wanting to sink to the floor and bury your face in your hands and sob until someone who loves you comes and puts a hand on your shoulder and makes it all better. There would have been someone like that in a kitchen like this, someone who would have made sure that little girls never cried alone.

To her left was a galley area crammed with old oak cupboards, sink on one side under a window, a cast-iron stove squatting on the opposite wall. Its fat oven door looked like a mouth, smugly closed over the memories of all the bread and pies and cookies it had once held inside. Straight ahead was a round wooden table with matching ladder-back chairs, all tucked neatly in an alcove cradled by a bay window. And everywhere there were reminders of the woman who had made this house a home—in the empty clay pots on the window-sill that might once have held aromatic herbs; in the tiny stitchwork of a wall-hanging that said 'Cooking is Love'.

'Madeline?' There was concern in his voice as he repeated, 'Is anything wrong?'

She turned her head slowly to look at him, mask back in place, her expression cool and detached. 'No. Of course not.'

When she turned back, she noticed a thin layer of dust on everything; a musty odour that advertised an empty house. No one had lived here for a very long time, she realised, and if the kitchen seemed to tremble with sleeping life it was just an illusion.

'No one's actually lived in this house for years,' Elias said, almost as if he'd read her thoughts. He passed her and walked over to stand at the sink, his eyes fixed on a distant

point outside the dull glass of the kitchen
window.

'I thought you lived here.'

His head jerked towards her in a snap that
sent his hair flying across his brow in a black
comma. 'No. Not here. I'll show you where.'

She followed him through the galley to a tiny
mud-room, then out through a back door. They
were met by a brick path that led them on a
meandering voyage through the back yard,
passing the eerie skeletal remains of hundreds
of roses.

'Are they dead?' Madeline asked, feeling a
strange sympathy for the stiff black sticks that
poked up through the dead mess of compacted
leaves and dried grass.

'I don't know,' he said brusquely over his
shoulder, walking even faster. 'Some are, and
some aren't.'

Suddenly the path made an abrupt turn to the
right, passed through a narrow opening in a
stand of white pine, and disappeared under the
wild grass of an open meadow. Less than
twenty yards ahead a white-framed building
much larger than the house seemed to pop from
the ground.

'*This* is where I live,' Elias said, pulling a key
from his pocket and opening the front door. 'I
had it built a few years ago.'

Madeline felt the firmness of short-napped
carpet under her heels as she walked a few steps
into the huge open space and turned in a slow
circle. The building had no interior walls, no

furnishings, no windows—nothing to distract the mind or distort the sound.

Of course this was where he lived. If she'd thought about it at all, she would have realised that he no longer belonged in the house of his youth. But this—this was just the kind of uninterrupted starkness that fostered genius, and let it flow unimpeded.

There was an enormous Steinway concert grand on a raised platform in the centre of the building's open interior. Her eyes touched the piano with something like reverence, then shifted to the grey acoustic tile climbing the walls and the rafters to the peak of the roof, creating a perfect chamber for the sound that would rise from below. Her fingers twitched with an almost uncontrollable need to run to the piano and play; to make music in a place designed for that and nothing else. Behind her, Elias watched her hands at her sides and smiled coldly.

'Your studio,' Madeline whispered, hearing the sound of her voice absorbed instantly.

'And my home.' He led her to the far wall and pushed on a portion of the thick tile that had covered a door. Madeline walked through into a long narrow room that ran the entire length of the building. It had a desk with a work-light, a bed, a dresser, and little else.

'There's a small kitchenette back there,' he nodded towards a door at the far end, 'and a bath, of course. Everything I need.' There was something decidedly unpleasant about his smile, as if he was forcing it.

Madeline backed out of the small room, finding it suddenly disturbing. 'You don't use the house at all?'

Elias closed the door with a faint smile. 'No. The house will be yours, for as long as you work for me.' He walked away towards the piano, never noticing that Madeline had frozen in place, her lips parted slightly.

The house would be hers, she thought, shivering. Not forever, but for a time, the house would be hers.

'Madeline?'

She blinked, focused on where he was leaning back against the piano, his elbows propped behind him, his eyes fixed on hers across the space between them. 'Come play for me,' he said quietly, and, without any warning at all, Madeline's heart turned over.

She looked at him from across the room, and something about the distance between them, or perhaps the added height of the platform, made him look taller, broader, almost god-like, and suddenly she was afraid. He pulled at her, just as the house pulled at her, waking old emotional responses from the grave of her childhood; and those responses terrified her.

She walked woodenly towards the platform, reeled in on the line between his eyes and hers, and, when she finally sat down at the piano, her hands were trembling.

The trembling stopped the moment she touched the keys.

Nearly fifteen minutes later her hands fell from the keyboard and she closed her eyes, feeling drained and empty.

'Thank you,' he whispered from behind and to her right, and she turned slowly on the bench to look up at green eyes as beautifully serene as the undisturbed surface of a woodland pond. There was a shadow of a smile on his lips.

'It sounded like that in my head, when I wrote it,' he said quietly, and Madeline realised that she had just played the overture from an Elias Shepherd musical that no one would produce. Too ponderous, the critics had said; too mechanical; and, with that, the down-slide of his popularity had begun. She couldn't recall deciding to play it; only that the notes had flowed from her fingers to the keyboard, as if that was the piece she had been destined to play on this particular occasion.

'Anything you want, Madeline,' he was saying earnestly, moving closer to her now, bringing all the heat of the room with him, passing that heat through his hands to her shoulders when they finally rested there. 'I'll give anything to have the world hear my music the way you play it.'

She stared straight ahead, her thoughts racing. All of her life she had wanted things from other people, but had had nothing to give in return. At last, someone wanted *her*; at last, she had something someone thought was valuable, and for the first time she experienced that tremulous wonder of being a participant in the human race, instead of simply an onlooker.

Let me live in that wonderful old house, let me play your music, let me be close to you while you work—let me have that forever, she was thinking; but she knew better than to ask for forever.

'You and I aren't going to win any prizes for tough negotiating,' she said, pretending to be amused. 'I'll do anything to play your music, and you'll do anything to see that I do.'

He chuckled softly and moved his hands on her shoulders, turning her to face him, dropping to his heels next to the bench and looking directly up into her eyes. 'We're a perfect match, you know—two people who don't give a damn for anything but music; but for the music we'll sacrifice anything. We should make a hell of a team.'

Her smile felt a little weak. 'Yes. We should.' But it won't last, a little voice taunted her, because you want it too much, and when you want things, or need them, or, God forbid, learn to love them, they disappear.

She tensed when his hands slid down her arms to her wrists, brushing against the soft swell of her breasts on the way. He turned her hands palm up in her lap, cradling them in his, gazing at them with such an expression of awe that she felt strangely detached from them, as if they were a separate entity he worshipped, one that had nothing to do with her as a person. Something about that troubled her, but, before she had time to analyse it, his hair was brushing against the soft flesh of her inner arm, his lips were grazing the inside of her wrist, and all reasonable thoughts fled in the face of intense physical sensation.

She stared down at where his head was bent over her, marvelling that the pressure of his mouth on her wrist should have such a startling effect on the rest of her body. A dark, sleeping coil of heat began to unwind in the pit of her stomach, its fiery warmth spreading down to her legs, up to her chest and face in a visible flush, and she felt her breath come faster.

This is it, she thought, mesmerised. This is the poetry and the music and the meaning of life, and you're feeling it for the very first time. Hold still. Hold your breath, and maybe it will never end.

Suddenly he rose and pulled her to her feet, drawing her slowly against him, and for the first time in her life Madeline felt the full length of a man's body pressed against hers.

'Look at me, Madeline,' he whispered, pulling back slightly, his voice hoarse and dark and somehow frightening; drawn as tight as the muscles in the arms that held her.

She raised her eyes obediently, caught her breath when she saw that his had darkened; that by some peculiar trick of the light they looked black rather than green, and very, very hot.

'Elias.' The word was merely a quick expulsion of breath as their eyes met, and, though she had never said the name before, it felt familiar passing over her lips.

Later she would wonder if saying his name aloud had shattered some strange, magical spell, because in the next instant he stiffened abruptly and stared at her in shock, as if he'd just realised who he was holding in his arms. The skin around his eyes tightened and he held her at arm's length, as afraid to hold on as he was to let go. 'I'm sorry,' he said, his voice strained. 'I don't know what made me do that. Maybe David's right. Maybe I've been alone for too long.'

The words were like cold, dark fingers tightening around her heart. Was that all it had been? No poetry, no music, no profound connection decreed by destiny? Just the impulsive act of a man too long alone?

She searched his eyes long enough to see a plain, colourless creature reflected there, and didn't wonder that he had pulled away.

Her expression blank, arms hanging limply at her sides, she watched him take a few quick steps away, then turn back.

He stared at her for a moment, his gaze steady now, his expression unreadable. 'It's late,' he said finally, turning for the door. 'We'd better get back to the city.'

Madeline sat in numbed silence during the ride home. In broken, hesitant spurts of awkward conversation, Elias offered her an outrageous salary, even the promise of future royalties, and Madeline simply nodded in wordless agreement. None of it mattered; none of it had anything to do with why she would go to Rosewood.

# CHAPTER FOUR

For the next three days Madeline occupied every waking moment with a flurry of activity. She washed and ironed and packed her meagre wardrobe, rescheduled all her students with other piano teachers, cleaned her apartment in preparation for a long absence—anything to keep her mind busy and the memory of that moment in the studio safely buried. But occasionally a sharp, unexpected flash of memory would catch her by surprise, interrupting her work, and at those moments she would stop and grit her teeth, fighting to forget the heart-stopping sensation of being caught in Elias's embrace.

Again and again, especially at night when she lay exhausted yet unable to sleep, she replayed those few precious moments in her mind. Elias had touched her, and with that touch he had shattered her defences, made her hope for things she'd always known would never be hers. And then he'd simply pulled away, unaffected by the act that had moved her world. To him it had been merely a momentary lapse—a simple physical reaction that had no more meaning than the drawing of a breath. In a way, she hated him for that; hated him because she was tormented by the memory of his touch, while all that tormented him was how long it was taking her to pack.

He called from David's every day, and with each successive call his voice sounded more impatient. 'What the hell is taking so long?' he'd exploded through the wires just this morning, and something inside Madeline had snapped.

'I have a life!' she'd shouted back, her knuckles whitening on the receiver. 'It takes some time to shut down a life, you know!' And then she'd hung up on him in a gesture of defiance so totally unlike her that even now, hours later, she could hardly believe she'd done it.

She sat, exhausted, on the couch in her darkened living-room, her hands curled around a coffee-cup long since empty, trying to muster enough energy to get up and drag herself into bed. She jumped when the phone rang on the stand next to her.

'Madeline.'

Her eyes fluttered closed at the sound of his voice and she answered quietly. 'Yes.'

'I called to apologise, Madeline. I was impatient this morning. I'm sorry.' After a moment's silence he said, 'Madeline? Are you still there?'

'I'm sorry about this morning, too,' she mumbled finally. 'I shouldn't have hung up on you.'

'Don't be silly. I had it coming. David's spent the entire day calling me four kinds of a tyrant for being so impatient, and he's absolutely right.'

One corner of her mouth turned up in a rueful smile. She'd spent little more than five minutes with him, and already David had become her self-appointed champion. 'Thank him for me,' she said quietly.

'You can thank him yourself. I'm sure he'll come up to Rosewood to visit us occasionally—unless. . .you haven't changed your mind about working for me, have you?'

The question startled her, because she had never considered changing her mind, but hearing it spoken aloud made her realise that she should have; that she was setting herself up for yet another disappointment. She was going to fall in love again with another place she had to leave behind.

Suddenly she straightened and grasped the phone even more tightly, and her expression grew hard. It didn't have to be that way. Not this time. All she had to do was remain detached—from everything—and she'd had years of practice at that. She did it very well.

'No,' she said at last. 'I haven't changed my mind.'

'How much more time do you need to wrap up your affairs here?'

She glanced at the stack of suitcases by the door, the completed list of things to do at her right hand, the cover on her piano that looked ominously like a shroud. 'I'm finished,' she said tiredly, anticipating one more night in her own bed, wondering if she'd lie awake for hours again.

'I'll be there in twenty minutes.'

He hung up before she could protest that it was already ten o'clock; that there was no reason to drive two hours in the dark when they could just as easily wait until morning. . .

She rang back immediately, but no one answered, and within an hour they were in the car and speeding north.

She slept all the way to Rosewood, and only woke up enough to stumble groggily up the narrow stairs of the gingerbread house, Elias supporting her with an impersonal hand under her elbow.

She never noticed the soft gleam of newly polished wood, reflecting the moonlight that streamed through the bedroom window; and she wasn't consciously aware of the fresh-air smell of sheets dried in the sun and wind; but she did smile a little as she burrowed her head deep into the feather pillow, and that night she dreamed of roses.

The next sounds she heard were terrifyingly unfamiliar—a harsh, croaking scream, a low, vibrant moaning that went on and on. Her eyes flew open and focused on the cross-hatched beams of a strange ceiling, and when the sounds came again she closed her eyes and laughed silently at herself. She would have slept through the wail of a siren or the blaring horns of traffic or the muted shouts of voices rising in anger from the street—but not through the morning call of a rooster or the lowing of a distant cow.

You're in the country now, she reminded herself, wondering if she had ever slept so soundly before. No street noises, no neighbours arguing through the thin walls of her apartment, no throbbing stereos jingling the glass bottles on her dressing-table. . . She flung the down duvet back and shivered when the cool air hit her body—and no nightgown, either, she reminded herself wryly, sitting up and rubbing vigorously at her arms. She had a vague memory of shaking her head when Elias asked last night if she had wanted her suitcase; an even vaguer memory of stripping down and crawling naked into bed. She turned to grab her clothes from the bedside chair, and then froze.

Elias was standing in the doorway, one leg stopped in mid-stride, a forgotten breakfast tray tipping dangerously in his hands. His eyes raced down and up the length of her body, then fixed on her face in mute surprise.

For a moment they were both part of a motionless tableau, two equally astonished human beings staring into each other's eyes, because they were afraid to look anywhere else. Madeline was the first to move, snatching the duvet up over her breasts.

He glanced at where her hands clutched at the duvet, then back up to her wide, startled

52  HEARTSONG

eyes. 'Sorry.' He walked quickly over to place the tray on the bedside table.

Madeline sat with her mouth still open, her face so hot it felt like it was on fire, watching every move he made. When she finally managed to find her voice, she blurted out, 'You told me you lived in the studio, that the house would be mine. . .'

He lifted one shoulder in a casual shrug that seemed to dismiss her nakedness as barely worthy of note. 'A welcoming breakfast seemed appropriate for your first day.' He flicked a checked napkin from the tray, and the aroma of coffee and eggs filled the room. 'Sorry if I embarrassed you. I was sure you'd be up and dressed by now. Enjoy your meal. I'll see you downstairs.'

She lay motionless in the bed for a long time after he left, numbed by his reaction. Not that she expected any man would ever be moved to passion by the sight of her body, of course, but neither had she expected such monumental indifference from the first one who ever saw her naked.

It was worse than humiliating; it was like being negated right out of existence. He hadn't seen her at all. It seemed to substantiate that the one time he had been moved to respond to her as a woman, it had been almost unintentional.

It wasn't like Madeline to get angry—anger was one of the first emotions to go when you started discarding them all as counterproductive—and the truth was it wasn't even appropriate now. You didn't get angry because a man *didn't* attempt an assault; that was just plain sick. Still, the whole episode was unsettling. A lascivious leer would have been better than his chilling indifference, she thought; and then she blushed furiously for thinking such a thing at all.

Irritated at herself as much as him, she flung the duvet aside and got out of bed, attacking the suitcases that had somehow found their way upstairs to her room. Before she knew what she was doing, almost every article of clothing she owned lay crumpled where she'd flung it across the room. Appalled by her own behaviour, at the visible evidence of emotions she hadn't realised she had, she dressed in an old pair of jeans and a paint-spattered T-shirt she'd brought along to use as a dust rag. She'd be damned if she'd take any care to dress for a man who barely noticed her presence.

'You *are* a fashion plate, aren't you?' he asked, barely suppressing a wry smile when she stomped into the kitchen.

'I don't know why I bothered to dress at all,' she said sarcastically. 'Seems like a pretty pointless effort, if you're going to come popping into my bedroom all the time.' She slammed the breakfast tray down on the work-top and watched little balls of scrambled eggs jump from the plate. She hadn't even tasted them.

'Oh, for crying out loud,' he said, exasperated. 'I said I was sorry if I embarrassed you. So I saw you naked. So what? It's not as though I took pictures to sell on the street corner.'

She turned her back on him, ostensibly to pour herself a fresh cup of coffee, but actually to hide the confusion on her face. She wasn't a bit angry that he'd walked in on her; she was angry because it hadn't affected him, and what kind of a woman did that make her?

'Madeline?'

'What.' Even when the silence became long and awkward, she didn't turn around to look at him.

'Madeline,' he repeated, and his tone was softer now. 'I didn't mean to offend you. The truth is I rushed you in the city, and I had no right to do that. Bringing up your breakfast was supposed to be a peace offering, not an invasion of privacy.'

Madeline released a long, frustrated sigh. He was trying to apologise, and it would probably be much better in the long run if he never knew he was apologising for the wrong thing.

She took her coffee over to the table and sat down opposite him. He was wearing jeans, she noticed, and the sleeves of his white shirt were pushed up to expose a muscular forearm. She wondered how one developed a forearm like that, sitting at a piano all day. 'It doesn't matter,' she sighed. 'I over-reacted. Let's forget it.'

The tight smile flashed on and off his face so fast she wasn't sure it had ever been there.

'I didn't know you cooked,' she said, looking out of the window so she wouldn't have to meet his eyes.

'Only under duress. We could have gone out for breakfast, but this morning I didn't want to waste the time. I'd like to get right out to the studio and get to work.'

Madeline's cup rattled in its saucer. 'Today? But I haven't even unpacked yet, or organised my room, and if I'm going to live in this place it's going to need a little cleaning.' She dragged her finger through the dust on the table and held it up for his inspection.

He shook his head. 'Becky will take care of all that.'

'Becky?'

He nodded and his smile warmed his face. 'You'll love Becky. She lives in the village, but she'll be out every day to cook, clean, do whatever needs doing. . .' He raised a dark brow at her troubled expression. 'Surely you didn't think you were coming up here to keep house? You won't have time for that sort of thing. We have too much to accomplish in too little time.'

Madeline watched him as he rambled on, noticing how rapidly he drank his coffee, how rapidly he did *everything*, as if life were too short to pause and savour its pleasures.

'We have to have a rough score, or at least the overture, ready for the producer by the month's end, and, if he likes it, that's when the pressure will really start. Another month, two at the outside, to finish the soundtrack, then record it; then we might be asked to do some publicity performances to promote the film, or even a full-scale tour, and that's just the beginning. . . Think you can handle it?'

She shook her head rapidly, horrified at the thought. 'I'm not a performer. I'm just a piano teacher. I told you that. I've never performed. I've never wanted to perform. I couldn't possibly do publicity spots or tours or——'

'You were born to perform.' He was looking directly into her eyes, making that deep, frightening connection she felt when she played his music; a connection that made a lie of his earlier indifference.

Suddenly he frowned, then jerked his eyes away as if he realised they might be revealing too much. 'Drink your coffee,' he said brusquely, 'and we'll go make some music.'

# CHAPTER FIVE

MADELINE stopped just outside the kitchen door, stunned by the change in the back yard in just three days. Like a tardy actress bursting upon the scene, finally remembering where she was supposed to be, spring had exploded on the stage of the country.

The lilac bushes she remembered as barely dressed skeletons were now fully clothed, lining the yard like an eager crowd on a parade route, proudly waving their glossy new leaves. Behind them, towering cottonwoods poked greening arms into the serene blue of the sky, and, from somewhere close by, apple trees sent the sweet fragrance of new blossoms wafting through the air. Even the graveyard of roses seemed less stark, less black and white, as if the promise of life quivered there in a hint of colour barely seen.

Turn the soil, prune back a little dead wood, and the rose garden could be beautiful, she mused, mesmerised by the fantasy image of hundreds of flowers coming to life under her hands. How many years had she coddled stunted house-plants in her tiny apartment, dreaming of a garden just like this? It was all she could do to keep from dropping to her knees and digging her bare hands into the still chilled earth.

'Coming?' Elias had stopped a few paces ahead on the path to glance over his shoulder at her. She lifted her eyes from the make-believe garden and looked at him, and perhaps her expression reflected a fleeting trace of the beauty of her vision, because he caught his breath and froze where he stood.

The sun glanced off his dark hair in bluish flashes of light; it pierced the thin white of his shirt to outline the hard body beneath; and without any warning at all she felt herself taking possession of the man and the garden, as if they both belonged to her now, and always had.

Fantasy, her thoughts stumbled, trying to be realistic, but her eyes remained wide and fixed on his, her lips slightly parted, for it seemed that she was seeing at last the visualisation of that indefinable something that had first pulled at her from Rosewood; that vague promise of something wondrous that had compelled her to defy reason and bind herself to a man and a place she would have to leave eventually.

'You're lovely, standing there,' he said quietly, barely moving his lips. Then a shadow seemed to darken his features, and he turned slowly—reluctantly, she thought—and began to walk again.

She followed him, trance-like, along the path, through the naked roses to the break in the pines and across the field to the studio building.

She was hardly aware of arriving at their destination at all, so transfixed was she by the way his shoulder-blades shifted under his shirt, the way dark tendrils of hair lifted from his head to greet the breeze. The sun warmed her back through the T-shirt, the air cradled her in a fragrant envelope of new life, and Elias Shepherd thought she was lovely. The world seemed to be smiling on the first day of her new life, and, if omens could be found in things as simple as weather and environment, the future held nothing but promise.

And then they entered the studio, and everything changed.

The moment the door sighed closed behind them, Madeline sensed a subtle difference, as if the building itself were effecting a transformation on Elias every bit as powerful as that of spring upon the world. She glanced at his face and saw a strange sharpness there, and knew, without understanding how she knew, that the man in the garden—the man who had called her lovely—had not survived the passage through the studio door. The rigid, preoccupied man at her side barely resembled him at all.

Without warning he looked down at her abruptly, his eyes stopping on hers, the rich green flaring briefly with a dark light that made her tremble. Then just as quickly he looked up again and stared across the room at the piano, and suddenly Madeline felt herself start to disappear. 'I can almost hear the music,' he murmured. His gaze was still fixed on the concert grand, then, just when she was least expecting it, his head snapped around and he glared at her.

She frowned at the unfamiliar expression in his eyes, then paled when she recognised it as hostility. My God! What had she done to deserve that?

'Go on,' he said harshly. 'You're wasting time.'

She blinked once in confusion, as if the world had suddenly slipped out of focus.

'You heard me!' he barked when she didn't move. 'Don't just stand there gaping. We've got work to do. Now get over to the piano and warm up.' And then he spun on his heel and stalked across the room towards his living quarters.

Madeline just stared after him, totally bewildered by his behaviour; so bewildered, in fact, that she wondered if he had really spoken that harshly, or if she had only imagined it. She rubbed her hands slowly up and down her arms, feeling suddenly chilled, and made her way over to the piano.

Her fingers automatically found the keys and shattered the quiet with the comforting, familiar noise of minor scales pounded out in full octaves. She played harder and harder, faster and faster, eventually drowning out the echo of his voice in her mind.

She closed her eyes and let her stiffened

hands range over the piano, striking like minia-
ture two-legged tables until the very air around
her shuddered sympathetically. Her head
bobbed in jerky counterpoint, her lips melded
into a thin white line, and only when the tension
of rigid muscles screamed for relief did she free
her fingers to race up and down in rapid scales
that brought blood rushing into her hands.

'All right. That's enough.'

Her hands froze over the keyboard. She
sensed his presence just behind her right
shoulder, and wondered absently how he had
got there without her noticing.

'Here.' A rectangle of white appeared in the
blurred tunnel of her vision. 'Play this.'

She winced at the tone of command in his
voice, and her grey eyes darkened to the colour
of gathering storm clouds. Her hands remained
motionless over the keys.

'Breathe.'

She jumped at the pressure of his hands on
either side of her neck.

'Breathe, I said.'

For one crazy instant her resolve was firm
never to breathe again, simply because that was
what he had told her to do, but then she pulled
in air with a gasp, frustrated that her body had
betrayed her will so quickly. Her lungs filled,
emptied raggedly, then filled again as his fingers
pushed deep into the knotted muscles and
began to knead.

'Don't do that.' She tried to shrug off his hands, but they just kept coming back.

'Hush. Be still. Relax.' His voice was husky, as hypnotic as his hands, and the hostility, if it had ever been there, was gone. Perhaps she *had* imagined it all, like a bad dream.

She felt the tension start to bleed away, felt her shoulders start to sag, and gradually her hands lowered to the keyboard, depressing the keys without making a sound.

'There.' The hands left her neck. 'That's better. Now play.'

Almost mindlessly, she focused on the staff paper propped up in front of her and began to play.

As she came to the end of the first sheet, another appeared magically; and then another, and another, and she played on, her brows tipped in inexpressible sadness, her lips parted in an unspoken sigh. At some point she ceased to merely play the music, and somehow *became* the music; and the haunting, heart-breaking melody that rose from the piano was nothing less than the song of her own heart.

At last she struck a particular pianissimo chord that seemed to be waiting for something, but there were no more sheets, no more notes to play. The sound of that chord hung in the air long after her hands had fallen to her lap.

She felt a gentle pressure on her chin, turning her head to the right, and it took her a moment to recognise the pressure as a hand. At some point Elias had moved to sit next to her on the bench, and now his fingers were cupping her chin and he was staring at her, his eyes quietly intent.

'For the movie?' she murmured.

He nodded. 'The title song. I started writing it the night we met.'

She pressed her lips together and tired to fight the sudden rush of warmth that felt strangely like an embrace. It had been so intimate, playing his music, feeling his music, trespassing into the despair that had put those notes on paper, as if only she could enter his mind and tell the world what she had seen there. The bond of such a thing was overwhelming. . .and terrifying.

He felt it, too—the wild surge of joy, and the terror as well. She could see it in his eyes, sense it in the heated tremble of his fingers as they slipped from her chin to her neck, then down to the pulse in the hollow of her throat.

She was dimly aware that his hand was moving down towards the rise of her breast, and in a separate compartment of her mind an unheard voice cried out a warning—pull away, Madeline; pull away now, while there's still time—but she was lost in the green of his eyes that promised spring and rebirth, and her breast throbbed under his hand like the earth warming under the morning sun.

It all seemed so natural, so inevitable. She had belonged to Elias Shepherd ever since she'd first played his music, and, just as surely, he had belonged to her.

Instinctively she raised her hand to cover his, to press it more firmly against her breast, and for a moment she thought he was smiling at her, somewhere behind the steady eyes and the set mouth, somewhere deep inside where no one else could see; but then suddenly his expression darkened with something like alarm, he snatched his hand away, and shot up from the piano bench and glared down at her.

Before she could make sense of what was happening, he had turned back to the first sheet of music and was jabbing at it with one finger. 'Play it again!' he demanded.

Frowning, she looked back at the music, but the notes seemed to blur together on the page.

'Play,' he commanded her again, and her brows twitched a little, as if she recognised the word but couldn't quite remember the proper response.

'Dammit, *play*,' he spat, and her hands moved tentatively to the keyboard, remembering what was required even if her brain didn't. The first chord rang sharply discordant.

'B *flat*!' he bellowed, startling her so badly that she bit down on her tongue. 'For God's sake, that's a B flat!'

He was yelling at her. The bastard was yelling at her. She didn't have to take that, of course, and she wouldn't. Just as soon as she was thinking just a little more clearly, just as soon as

she found her voice again, she would tell him
that.

He began to snap his fingers right next to her
ear, trying to force her to pick up the tempo.
'Come on, come *on*,' he said irritably. 'You
played it perfectly the first time; what's the
matter with you? You sound like a first-year
student. Concentrate!'

She concentrated. It was better to concentrate
on the music than on his sudden, inexplicable
hostility; better than thinking about what had
happened between them, or almost happened,
or had she imagined it all? Her hands started to
come down harder on the keys, faster, splinter-
ing the air with the raucous complaint of mis-
played notes, and oddly enough she didn't care.
As a matter of fact, there was a perverse satisfaction in playing it all wrong, in making a terrible,
ghastly noise that would drive him——

'What is this?' He had to shout to be heard
over her banging. '*Jump* into that phrase! *Flutter*
the trill! Dammit, what the hell are you doing?'

And suddenly, it was enough. She slammed
both hands forcefully down on the keyboard,
jumped to her feet, and spun to face him, her
face red, her eyes flashing. For the first time in
her life Madeline felt the stirrings of real defiance. She wanted to shout at him; to pound
her fists against his chest and scream that she
didn't understand, that it didn't make sense that
he kept offering the teasing promise of affection
only to pull back, just as life had always offered

things like home and family and then snatched
them away. . .

But Madeline wasn't good at defiance. She'd
never been taught that she had the right to
shout and pound her fists and question the way
others treated her when it seemed unfair; so,
when she finally spoke, her voice was flat and
dull. 'I don't think we'll be able to work together
after all,' she said simply. 'You'd better find
someone else.'

She had a brief glimpse of emerald eyes flying
wide in surprise before she pushed past him
and left the studio, but once safely outside she
sagged heavily against the door to keep her
knees from buckling under her.

Oh, lord, it had been an awful mistake; such
an awful mistake to come here; to subcon-
sciously hope that relating to the man's music
would mean she could relate to the man as well.

She pushed herself away from the door and
stood erect, thinking that perhaps she was
stronger than she thought. At least this time she
was leaving on her own, before someone sent
her away. As she started to walk back towards
the house, her mind clutched at this new-found
shred of pride, trailing behind her like the rem-
nant of a wispy cloud.

# CHAPTER SIX

MADELINE fumbled through the kitchen cupboards until she'd found the makings for another pot of coffee, then sat at the kitchen table, staring out at the rose garden, feeling every bit as dead as the black sticks that jutted from the earth. Walking out on Elias's fit of temper might have satisfied her pride, but there wasn't much residual warmth to the feeling.

She stiffened in her chair when she saw him coming towards the house, his hands clasped behind his back, his head bent as if he was deep in thought. She hated her sharp awareness of him as a man, her weakness in noticing the way his jeans moulded themselves to his legs as he walked, in seeing the breadth of his shoulders and the sunlight glancing off the lighter strands in his dark hair.

He came through the door quietly, met her eyes, then slid into the chair opposite her at the table. 'Maddie,' he said softly, and she frowned, suspicious of his gentle tone, and of the nickname. No one had ever called her that before. 'I don't blame you for walking out on me out there; I had it coming. But I don't want to get another pianist. I *can't* get another pianist. Not like you.'

She felt the traitorous, involuntary flutter of her heart inside her chest, as if a tiny sparrow were trapped there.

'I'm sorry about what happened out there. I don't have a single excuse for treating you the way I did. God knows you deserve better——' He stopped abruptly, rubbing his hand over his mouth.

'Are you apologising for the way you touched me, or the way you yelled at me afterwards?' The words were out of her mouth before she realised she was going to say them, and her heart jumped to her throat, they sounded so bold.

He'd frozen in place at her question, his eyes fixed on hers. 'Both,' he said quietly. 'I had no right to do either.'

Oh, but you did, she was thinking. I gave you the right to touch me that way, in my heart, at least. . .

He was still motionless; still staring at her. 'I got involved with my pianist once before, Madeline; married her, in fact.' He smiled bitterly.

Madeline took a mental step backwards, wondering why David hadn't told her Elias's wife had also been his pianist.

'We both loved the music,' Elias continued in a dull monotone, 'and I was fool enough to think that meant we loved each other. Getting those two things confused turned out to be a disaster, and I'm not about to make the same mistake again.'

In his eyes Madeline saw a reflection of the same pain she'd seen in her mirror for years; the same brittle defence she herself had erected against the temptation to let someone in, to risk that pain again. No wonder he'd become so suddenly cold when they'd entered the studio to work.

He looked away abruptly, as if he couldn't bear the sight of her face for too long at one time.

'I'm not your ex-wife,' she reminded him gently.

He looked straight into her eyes, and something he saw there made his features relax. 'No, you're not.' After a moment, his mouth trembled with the beginnings of a smile. 'You're magic, Madeline, and you don't even know it, do you?'

She remembered David calling her that the day they'd met—magic Madeline, he'd said— had Elias called her that first? She felt a prickle behind her eyes and blinked hard.

'I didn't just divorce my wife,' he said softly. 'I think I divorced the whole world. I hid myself away for so long, I think I'd almost forgotten how to care, how to *feel*. . .and then I heard you play my music that day, I heard you playing your feelings out loud on the piano, and. . .it was like hearing my feelings, too; reminding me I had them.'

His smile was heart-breakingly tender as he reached across the table and captured both her hands in his. 'It was like waking up after a long sleep. You made me come alive again, Maddie. It's as simple as that.'

Madeline sat perfectly motionless, barely breathing, her fingers trembling against his palms.

'Something happens when you play my music, Maddie; some spiritual connection so powerful that it makes the music come to life, too. It's so rare; such a precious thing. . .' His brows angled like two black wings shadowing his eyes. 'I won't let that be destroyed.'

She blinked in confusion, dark lashes battering the pale rise of her cheeks.

'Relationships don't last forever, Madeline.'

She nodded woodenly. No one knew that better than she did.

'But our music will.' His eyes seemed strangely bright, almost iridescent. 'The music you and I make together might just last forever, if we don't destroy it by giving in to something that wouldn't last nearly as long.'

Madeline felt the world pause for a moment, and in that pause something dark moved into the space between them. She felt her face stiffening, freezing into whatever expression she happened to be wearing.

'Maddie.' He tightened his fingers on hers and leaned across the table towards her, commanding her attention. 'Give me another chance.' The words were so softly spoken she could barely hear them.

She glanced down at where her hands were trapped like two lifeless birds, then looked up at him again with a faint, sad smile. 'For the music,' she said tonelessly.

'Yes. The music. Nothing is as important as that.'

Certainly not a moment of heedless, thoughtless passion, she thought bitterly; but then she let the bitterness seep away, because it was the music that had brought her into his life, and it was the music that would allow her to stay.

The little clock above the sink filled the silent kitchen with its ticking while Madeline closed her eyes and took a deep breath. 'The music is important to me, too,' she said softly, and his head jerked hopefully. A single black strand of hair separated from its fellows and dropped over his forehead.

'Does that mean you'll stay?'

Madeline looked down at her hands with a sigh of resignation, wondering if she could really do this—if she could really spend day after endless day watching him, hearing his voice, feeling his presence, touching his mind through the keyboard, pretending, always pretending, that she didn't care any more than he did. Wouldn't it be easier to leave now? Of course it would. And then this would just be one more place in a long line of places where she had left behind a piece of her heart. 'Things will have to be different,' she said quietly. 'I won't be yelled at. I want you to treat me like. . .a friend.'

His shoulders sagged as he released a long breath. He held her eyes for a moment, then slowly, solemnly, he extended his hand across the table. 'All right, Madeline. I promise.'

Madeline hesitated, and, even though she knew she was opening herself to pain that would never quite go away, she accepted his hand, sealing the new bargain between them.

He rose slowly from the table, and, for a man who had just got precisely what he wanted, he looked strangely sad. 'Why don't you take the rest of the day to get settled,' he said, 'while I do some work alone in the studio? There's a piano in the front parlour if you feel like playing.' He reached for the doorknob, then turned and looked at her. 'You won't regret this, Madeline,' he added. 'I promise.'

She watched silently as he left, then turned to the window to follow him with her eyes as he passed through the rose garden and disappeared between the white pines. 'Yes, I will,' she whispered.

She didn't know how long she had been sitting there, still staring out of the window, when the sound of a car in the front drive finally brought her to her feet.

She walked through the house to the front door, opened it, and looked out on a battered station wagon with a starburst crack on the right side of the windscreen.

A woman, whose petite, voluptuous form looked as though it had been poured into its brief shorts and halter, slid out from behind the wheel. Her brown hair spilled over her shoulders in thick, lustrous waves, and when her dark eyes saw Madeline a smile lit up the perfect oval of her face.

'Hello!' A tanned, graceful arm lifted in a wave, then she bent to retrieve sacks of groceries from the car.

Madeline walked out to help, assuming this was the woman Elias had told her about, a little taken aback by her extraordinary beauty. 'Hello. I'm Madeline Chambers.'

The woman handed over a grocery bag with a grateful smile. 'You couldn't be anyone else, not the way Elias described you. He did tell you about me, didn'the?'

'Yes; you're Becky, right?'

'Right. Cook, housekeeper, shopper—whatever you two need.' She shrugged with good humour. 'Where is Eli, by the way?'

Madeline's smile faltered a little to hear the personal shortening of his name. 'He's. . .out in the studio.'

'Ah.' She grabbed the last bag and slammed the car door, then led the way back to the house. 'Wouldn't do to disturb him, then, would it? Good lord. Look at this place!' She stopped just inside the door and shook her head. 'It looks even worse in the daylight. You can almost taste the dust.'

'In the daylight?' Madeline trotted along behind her, down the hallway past the stairs to the kitchen.

Becky flashed a knowing grin over her shoulder. 'I cleaned your bedroom after dark, which ought to explain any dustballs I might have missed.'

'Oh, you didn't have to do that. . .'

'Yes, I did. Elias calls, I come running. That's the way it is. Just put that bag down on the work-top, will you? Have you had a chance to get settled yet?'

'No,' Madeline replied distractedly. 'I haven't even unpacked.' She pursed her lips in consternation, remembering the clothes scattered across her bedroom. 'Well, actually I did unpack, sort of.'

'Sort of?'

She shrugged, a little embarrassed. 'I threw everything I brought with me all over the bedroom. I think I had a fit.'

Becky chuckled as she pulled a comb from her pocket and pinned her hair on top of her head. 'That was Elias's doing, no doubt. He does that, you know. Makes other people want to throw things.' She looked for confirmation in Madeline's face, apparently found it, then gave her head a little exasperated shake.

Madeline watched as she started to unpack

the grocery bags, wondering why such a beautiful woman wasn't a model instead of a housekeeper. 'Do you have a lot of houses to take care of?'

'Good lord, no,' Becky laughed, plunging her hands into another bag. 'I don't do this for a living. I only do it for Elias. I teach during the school year. This is my summer vacation.'

Madeline took a mental step backwards, but Becky just prattled on, oblivious. 'I'm glad he's here to stay for a while this time. Usually he's up for a few days, then off to somewhere else—*anywhere* else.' She paused and looked at Madeline. 'I've been trying to talk him into moving back here permanently for years. Maybe with your help, I can convince him.'

Madeline paled and took a real step backwards this time, and suddenly everything started to make perfect sense. Becky didn't clean houses for a living, she only did it for Elias; Becky cleaned the bedroom after dark—what had she said? 'Elias calls, I come running'?—and now she was soliciting Madeline's help to get him to stay with her permanently. . .

'Anything wrong?' Becky was frowning at her expression.

'No. Nothing at all.' She forced a thin smile. 'I'll get out of your way now.'

The words announced much more than her intention to leave the kitchen, but Becky had no way of knowing that.

'I'll have some lunch ready in just a little

while,' she said amiably, crouching down in front of the open refrigerator door, then jerking back, her pretty nose wrinkled in distaste. 'Oof. Something died in there.' She looked up and her face brightened. 'I'll be here every day from now on, by the way, so let me know if there's anything you need.'

Madeline smiled stiffly and nodded, then excused herself and left the kitchen, suddenly desperate to find a piano and play.

Elias hadn't shown her the parlour on her first tour of the house, choosing simply to tap the sliding wooden doors on one wall of the living-room as they passed. She parted the doors now with an effort, then looked into what had to be the largest room on the ground floor.

There were a few pieces of comfortable furniture, a fireplace of white brick, and a wall covered with dozens of framed photographs she decided to examine later. For now, she was anxious to uncover the shrouded baby grand piano over by the bay window.

It surprised her a little to find the antique black Steinway in need of refinishing, with obvious gouges that showed bare wood and the tell-tale yellowing of ivory keys. It wasn't the kind of piano one would expect Elias Shepherd to keep in his home.

But this house isn't his home, she reminded herself; he refuses to even sleep here. Besides, a quick check confirmed that the instrument was well cared for on the inside, at least. It had a fine, resonant tone, and was perfectly tuned.

Without another thought she sat down and let the restful, almost mournful beginning of Beethoven's 'Moonlight Sonata' erase the world. Within the first few bars she had pushed all conscious thought to the far corners of her mind, and lost herself in the music.

The piano had always been her escape, her refuge from reality too harsh to face, her release from emotions too intense to keep locked inside. Ever since she'd first touched a keyboard the piano had spoken for her, celebrating her triumphs and her joys, keening her sorrows, mourning her despair. She had been painfully shy as a child, and expressing her feelings through the piano had been much easier than sharing them with people who were never around for very long anyway. It still was.

She stopped playing after the first movement of the sonata, letting the sorrowful tones hang undisturbed in the air, a flawless echo of her mood.

She looked up and saw Becky in the doorway, standing perfectly still, a duster hanging limply from one hand. 'I'd forgotten,' she said quietly. 'I'd forgotten what it was like to have music in this house again. It's been a long time.'

'Rebecca!' The booming voice might as well have been a peal of thunder shattering the solemn moment. Becky's head spun so fast on her shoulders that a shiny loop of hair flew from the comb and dangled over one ear.

'In here!' she called out, her face suddenly, brilliantly radiant.

Within seconds Elias was in the doorway, scooping Becky into his arms with a smile Madeline had never seen on his face before. 'You're too damn gorgeous for your own good, you know. And you just keep getting better.' He cupped her face in his hands and kissed her gently on her cheek. Then they just stood there, smiling into each other's eyes, as oblivious of Madeline as if she'd been another piece of furniture.

She swallowed, blinked, thinking that apparently his determination to avoid emotional involvement applied only to pianists, not housekeepers, or teachers, or whatever the hell Becky was. She cleared her throat nervously, feeling like a child whose wistful face was pressed against a sweet-shop window.

Elias turned his head in a jerk and noticed her for the first time. 'Oh. I didn't realise you were in here.' He draped one arm over Becky's shoulder. 'I take it you two have introduced yourselves already—why don't we all sit down and have some coffee?'

Madeline tried to smile, but she couldn't quite pull it off. 'Actually, I was just about to go upstairs. I wanted to try the piano first.'

'So try it.' Elias started to cross the room, but

she jumped to her feet before he'd taken his second step.

'I already did. It's great, but I'm really tired now. See you both later.'

She walked out calmly, casually, but the moment the stairwell blocked her from their view she took the steps two at a time. Elias called her name sharply just as she closed her bedroom door behind her, but she didn't answer. She sagged against the door and held her breath, waiting for him to call again, but it didn't happen.

The dressing-table faced her from across the room, and it was inevitable that Madeline would eventually focus on her reflection in the mirror. The figure she saw looked shapeless under the wrinkled T-shirt, juvenile, and oddly pathetic.

With a heavy sigh she pushed away from the door, crossed the room, and leaned so close to the mirror that her breath fogged the glass.

'You're invisible,' she whispered sadly. 'He can hear you play, but he can't see you, because you're invisible.'

## CHAPTER SEVEN

THE setting sun was washing the room with rose-coloured light by the time Madeline awakened, jerked to a sitting position on the bed, and checked her watch.

Four hours. Good lord—she'd slept for four hours, and no one had bothered to wake her. But then why would they? she thought ruefully as her mind replayed the image of Elias and Becky wrapped in each other's arms. Three's a crowd, and all that.

Suddenly she was desperately homesick, for her own apartment, her own furniture; a safe, familiar place where she knew she belonged. The first time she'd seen it, she'd thought Rosewood could be such a place. The house, the setting, even the winter-dead rose garden had seemed to call to her like old friends; but how foolish that seemed in retrospect. There was no place for her here.

She took as much time as possible showering, washing and drying her hair, dressing, then picking up the mess she'd made of the room— anything to postpone the inevitable trip downstairs, the inevitable confrontation with Elias and Becky that would remind her she was as much an outsider here as she was anywhere else.

Like a child with a security blanket, she found some comfort in the one article of clothing she loved almost to distraction. Worn thin from countless washings, the long white cotton dress fell in soft folds from a high neckline all the way down to her ankles. With full sleeves caught loosely at the wrist and only an optional sash to define the waist, it was almost a parody of virginal modesty, and she caught herself wondering if wearing it had been a subconscious effort to counter Becky's skimpy attire.

Becky. The memory of the woman's vibrant sensuality seemed to mock the pristine reflection she saw in the mirror, white from neck to ankle, with a cloud of hair that was almost colourless fluffed about her shoulders. Her hand moved automatically for eyeshadow and blusher—anything to give life to the pale translucence of her face—but then the folly of trying to emulate Becky's beauty struck her, and she left the make-up untouched. With no excuses left to keep her from joining the others, she left her bedroom and started down the stairs.

Elias was waiting in the late afternoon shadows at the bottom.

She faltered when she saw him, slowed, and finally stopped, looking down at Elias looking up, his hand gripping the banister, his face frozen in the strangest expression. His hair was shiny black, newly washed, tumbling in careless disarray over his forehead to angle across one brow.

His eyes held her, rendered her silent with a green that seemed deeper than ever, as if all the intensity of spring's debut were reflected there. Peripherally she noticed that he was dressed all in black, but that only served to emphasise his eyes, to draw her gaze to the only two spots of colour and hold it there.

Without uttering a single word, he lifted his hand slowly from the banister and held it out to her, and, without thinking, she took it.

Her fingers tingled when she slipped them into his palm, and, with her eyes locked on his, she took a step down towards him, then another. She stopped one step up, her face level with his, because she could go no farther. There was no room to stand between him and the first riser, but there must have been, because suddenly he was saying, 'Come on, Maddie,' in a low whisper, and then his hands circled her waist and he lifted her towards him without effort. For one endless, mind-boggling second her feet dangled in mid-air and her heart seemed to float above her body as surely as her legs floated above the floor, then he let her down slowly. He was very, very close, and at the precise moment that Madeline became acutely conscious of the pressure of his fingers at her waist, he dropped his hands and backed quickly away from her.

They both looked down at the floor at the same time, then up at each other hesitantly.

'You must be hungry,' he said quietly. 'You slept right through lunch.'

Madeline's head moved in a jerky nod, her eyes wide. Through some trick of memory, she imagined that she could still feel his hands at her waist.

'Come on.' He turned and led the way down the hall towards the kitchen, and she followed mindlessly, her eyes focused on where his shirt clung to the hollow between his shoulder-blades.

'Becky made supper for us before she left,' he said over his shoulder. 'I didn't think you'd want to go out tonight.'

She rubbed absently at her waist as she followed him, erasing the memory of his touch. 'Becky's gone?'

'Hours ago.'

The kitchen was filled with the long shadows of late afternoon, the air itself subdued with the gloom of twilight. The light over the sink was on, but there was not yet enough darkness for its glow to appear warm. Madeline stopped just inside the doorway and shivered, feeling a vague disquiet.

Becky's touch was everywhere. In the galley area to her left the work-tops shone from a recent scrubbing, as did the ancient stove. The window over the sink was polished, and the empty clay pots had been banished from the sill to somewhere out of sight. In the alcove to her right, an expanse of shiny floor stretched to the newly swept hearth on the far wall, and even the easy chairs flanking it seemed brighter. Directly ahead, the table under the rose garden window was laid for two, its surface gleaming between sunny yellow place-mats.

She remained motionless in the doorway of the transformed room while Elias went to stir something wonderfully aromatic simmering on the stove.

'I've decanted some wine,' he told her. 'Will you pour?'

She followed his gaze to the crystal carafe and matching glasses on the table. It was an exquisite, deeply faceted pattern, obviously expensive, and strangely out of place between the two place-settings of country crockery. She smiled as she poured, thinking how many contrasts she had found in the short time she'd been at Rosewood. Meticulous, loving needlework filling an empty, loveless house; Elias tender and warm, then brutally cold; a dead, untended rose garden in the lush surroundings of spring; and now dazzling imported crystal in a country kitchen.

Elias joined her at the table. 'Cheers,' he said perfunctorily, lifting his glass. 'According to Becky, we're supposed to finish the bottle before we even think about eating.'

Madeline sipped at the deep red liquid and slid into one of the ladder-backed wooden

chairs. It made her uncomfortable that he
remained standing, looking down at her. 'Is
whatever she made that bad?'

'No,' he chuckled. 'Becky's a marvellous
cook.'

Naturally, Madeline thought, drinkly deeply,
wondering if there was anything the remarkable
Becky *couldn't* do. Housekeeper, cook, shopper. . .probably a nuclear scientist in her spare
time.

'I take it you like the wine?'

Madeline shrugged, then glanced at her glass,
amazed to find it almost empty. 'I guess I must.'

Elias nodded, smiling, and walked back to the
stove. 'Becky thought you might. Help yourself
to more.'

Becky, Becky, Becky. Madeline wondered if
her smile looked as forced on the outside as it
felt from the inside, and she stopped her hand
when it reached automatically for the carafe.

Supper was painfully silent. Madeline spent
most of the meal in a shallow pretence of watching darkness creep up on the rose garden outside the window, avoiding Elias's eyes as much
as possible.

'We were supposed to get to know each other
tonight,' he said suddenly, startling her.

'What?'

He put his fork down on his plate with exag-
gerated care, and watched it for a long moment
as if he expected it to move on its own. 'That's
what the wine was for. Becky thought it might

be nice if we just relaxed a little together; had a pleasant, social evening.'

'Did she?' One of Madeline's light brows arched prettily.

He nodded grimly and met her eyes. 'As pleasant, social evenings go, this one hasn't exactly been memorable so far, has it?' he asked wryly, tapping at the generous level of wine in the carafe. 'Becky was right. We should have finished the bottle.'

It was fully dark by the time they'd finished washing and drying the dishes. The clean-up had seemed particularly awkward, as if they were two strangers trying to play house.

Just as she was hanging her damp drying towel on the rack by the stove, Madeline heard Elias release a noisy sigh. His back was towards her, and she turned to see him leaning over the sink, his arms braced stiffly on the work-tops to either side, his head bent.

It just wasn't fair that the light should hit him quite that way, she thought miserably, making his hair shimmer like a dark, liquid crown; highlighting the way his silk shirt clung to the musculature beneath, rippling with every breath.

'We're not exactly ideal companions, are we?' he said, turning to face her with a wry grin. 'If tonight is any example, you're just about as adept at socialising as I am.'

She smiled a little at that. 'I'm sorry. I've never been much of a conversationalist.'

'Don't apologise. I'm the same way.'

They both sighed at the same time, then mirrored each other's nervous smiles. Elias turned away and pretended to tighten a tap that didn't need tightening. 'David called this afternoon,' he said into the sink.

'Oh?' She forced her eyes down and plucked an imaginary thread from her sleeve.

'He wanted to come up and take you out to dinner on Friday.'

Suddenly the thought of seeing David, of having someone, just as Elias had Becky, was enormously appealing. There would be no awkward silences in an evening of his company. Silence was an enemy to people like David, something dark and frightening to be kept at bay at all costs. 'I think I'd like that. What time will he be here?'

He turned suddenly to face her, and there was something odd about his expression. 'He won't. I told him not to come.'

Madeline hesitated for a moment, confused. 'Why would you do that?'

'Because,' he began, frowning uncertainly, and at first she thought that was the only reason he would offer. 'Because. . . I didn't want anything interrupting our work just yet.'

'I have to eat anyway,' she reminded him sullenly.

He shook his head impatiently and looked off to one side. 'David's too distracting,' he said brusquely. 'I decided that the last thing you need is something that will distract you from the music.'

She was speechless for a moment while she tried to channel the sudden rush of disbelief into words. '*You* decided?' she finally managed to force out.

His eyes narrowed defensively, but he still refused to look at her. 'That's right. I think I know what's best in this case.'

Madeline looked down at where her hands were tightening into white fists even before she realised she was angry. He sounded like a pompous parent trying to justify an unfair curfew. 'You have no right to make decisions like that for me,' she said carefully, but behind the control of her voice she couldn't help thinking that it was all right for him to have Becky on a daily basis—and if anyone qualified as a 'distraction', she certainly did—but she wasn't even to be permitted one evening away from his control.

The more she thought about it, the more she seethed, and when she finally looked up her eyes had darkened to a stormy grey and her chin jutted rebelliously. 'I work for you,' she said in clipped, precise tones. 'You don't own me, and if I want to go out to dinner with someone else, that's exactly what I'll do. I'll call David myself tomorrow, and I *will* go out with him on Friday night.' Then she spun in a swirl of white and stalked out of the kitchen and down the hall. She made it halfway to the stairs before he caught up with her.

He didn't say anything; just grabbed her right arm from behind and spun her around with such force that she nearly lost her balance. And then, when he had her facing him, her eyes startled behind the screen of blonde that had flown across her face, he didn't seem to know quite what to do with her.

His brow furrowed with confusion and he dropped her arm immediately. 'We can go out on Friday night,' he said, his voice gruff. 'There's no need to call David all the way up here.'

'David obviously wanted to come,' she said petulantly, 'and I'd like to see him.'

He met her eyes then and, in a gesture that caught her by surprise, lifted one hand to smooth the hair away from her face so he could see her more clearly.

Her eyes closed involuntarily at his touch, then opened slowly. After a long, searching look into them, he spoke quietly. 'I see. Well. That's different, then, isn't it?' He took a step backwards, and lifted his hands, palm up, as if he had held her trapped momentarily, and was now setting her free. 'You were going somewhere, I think.'

Madeline opened her mouth, then hesitated, staring up into eyes that looked black in the dim light of the hallway. He tipped his head, as if he was trying to read her expression in the dark, then simply turned away and walked back to the kitchen.

She followed him with her eyes, watched him glance over his shoulder at the last moment.

'I'll work alone tomorrow morning,' he said tonelessly. 'Be in the studio after lunch.'

In the next moment she heard the outside kitchen door open, then close softly behind him.

# CHAPTER EIGHT

SPRING. Madeline's lips formed the word silently as she raised her bedroom window, then breathed in the warm, sweet air of morning. In less than a week it had become ritual, this daily opening of the window, pulling in a deep breath, trying to identify the new scents the world presented with each dawn. This morning the rich, earthy aroma of freshly turned soil wafted up from the garden beneath her, soil turned by her hands only yesterday, and that she had had even a small part in enhancing such a sensory wonder filled her with satisfaction.

In the city, spring had always seemed to slip past her when she wasn't looking. But here, in the country, the season literally exploded into being, inundating her senses with a flood of fragrance and colour that took her breath away.

I will cherish this particular spring for the rest of my life, Madeline thought. In spite of everything.

Life at Rosewood had settled into a rigid routine of time periods divided more by the emotions they elicited than the hours of the day. While Elias worked alone in the studio, Madeline spent her mornings in the rose garden, immersed in the mystical wonders of nature, soothed by its predictability. These were the hours of serenity, broken only by an occasional piercing thrust of joy so unexpected that it never failed to surprise her. These moments were prompted by something as simple, and as miraculous, as seeing the hint of green life in a stem thought dead.

The afternoons were spent in the studio with Elias, working, always working, playing first drafts of his music, then the revisions, over and over again while he ran his hands through his hair, scowling, forever unsatisfied. It was obvious he was caught in a circle of frustrated creativity, and had yet to find the way out. He stomped and paced and swore and broke pencils and tore papers, and yesterday he had even pounded his fist against the wall; but, to be fair, he had never taken his frustration out on her. Their conversations were limited strictly to the music, but whenever he addressed her he was careful to keep his tone pleasant, his temper in check.

It seemed like a million years since they had shared that first handshake and promised friendship, and in retrospect such a relationship seemed ludicrous. For all the hours they spent in each other's company, they never spoke of anything but music, and that remained the only connection between them. And now, even that was fading with the inexplicable damming of his creative flow. Lately Madeline had been troubled with the thought that perhaps her playing was to blame and soon he would have to replace her. The weaning process might have already begun.

For the past three days and nights Elias had remained holed up in the studio, refusing to come up to the house even for meals, avoiding her company as much as possible. She was living twenty-four hours a day within calling distance of another human being, and yet she had never felt more alone.

Becky still came daily to clean and prepare meals and, although her presence alleviated the silence of the house, Madeline was never comfortable with her. As if her striking looks and relationship with Elias hadn't been intimidating enough, lately Madeline sensed an undercurrent of hostility that hadn't been there before. Perhaps Elias had confided that his new pianist was stifling him somehow, and Becky's protective instincts were rising to the fore.

As if the thought had produced her, Madeline heard the sound of Becky's car pulling into the drive, then the front door opening and closing as she entered.

The corners of her mouth turned down involuntarily from just knowing she was in the house, and then she felt guilty for feeling such a thing. It wasn't Becky's fault that she'd been born beautiful; that Elias felt for her things he could never feel for her things he could never feel for Madeline. Madeline sighed, thinking of the covered lunch trays Becky carried out to the

studio each day while she ate alone in the house.
Becky rarely came back before a full hour had
passed, and it didn't take a great mind to imagine how the two of them spent that time.

By the time Madeline got downstairs, Becky
was on her hands and knees scrubbing the
kitchen floor, her dark hair pulled back under a
blue bandanna, her face flushed and shiny with
a sheen of perspiration. She wore the usual cut-
off jeans that Madeline had begun to think of as
her work uniform, today with a snug, sleeveless
T-shirt that might once have been red, but had
long since faded to a murky rose colour. As
ever, she looked absolutely stunning. She sat
back on her heels when Madeline came in and
wiped her forearm across her brow.

'Coffee's ready,' she said. 'I see you're plan-
ning another morning in the garden.'

Madeline fingered the pony-tail on top of her
head nervously as she glanced down at her own
worn jeans and baggy plaid shirt. 'There's a lot
to do out there.'

Becky tipped her head, remembering. 'Elias's
mother used to love that garden, just like you.'
She hesitated, smiling a little. 'She's probably
looking down at the old place now, grinning
from ear to ear because someone's finally taking
care of her roses.'

It was the first piece of personal information
Madeline had learned about the woman who
had made this house a home with her love, and
she chewed on her lower lip, wondering how

far she dared take it. 'Did you know her very well?'

Becky shook her head. 'Not as well as I would have liked. I only moved to Brighton Square a year before she died.'

'But you liked her.'

'I loved her,' Becky corrected her. 'She was an incredible woman.'

'I thought she was,' Madeline mused, thinking of all the times she'd felt that woman's loving presence in this house, in the garden. 'That's why I've never understood why Elias hates this house.'

Becky's eyes fixed on hers with a sudden intensity that was alarming. 'You don't know a thing about Elias, do you?'

It sounded almost like an accusation, and Madeline shook her head, feeling suddenly guilty for her ignorance.

'Well,' Becky said a little sharply, 'it's really up to him to tell you anything he wants you to know; not me.' She hesitated, then clicked her tongue a little, as if she regretted being so curt. 'I didn't mean to snap at you. Lord knows, you probably get more than enough of that working with Eli.'

Madeline looked down and mumbled. 'He doesn't do that so much any more. At least he tries not to. We reached an agreement.'

'So I heard,' she said flatly, looking down at the bucket of soapy water and sighing with exasperation. 'I couldn't believe it when Elias told me you'd agreed to be "friends".' She said the word derisively, as if being a friend to Madeline were beyond comprehension.

'You don't like me very much, do you?' The words were out of Madeline's mouth before she knew she was going to say them, and Becky glanced up sharply, surprised.

'I don't really know you,' she finally replied, and then her lovely dark brows came together in a frown as she studied Madeline. 'You remind me a little of his mother, you know. She was fair, as you are, and almost as cool.' Her eyes took in Madeline's outfit, and suddenly she chuckled. 'Of course she never would have been caught dead in that outfit. White hat, gloves and lawn dress—that was her style.'

'I shouldn't really wear white,' Madeline mumbled. 'I disappear.'

'That's not what Elias says.' She sighed again and bent back to her scrubbing just before Madeline's mouth dropped open. 'Of course women like you look good in just about anything. Always made me jealous as hell, to tell you the truth.'

Flabbergasted, Madeline stared down at the rich, glossy hair bouncing in time to Becky's vigorous arm movements. 'But you're so beautiful,' she whispered. 'You're the most beautiful woman I've ever seen.'

Becky sat back on her heels again and looked at her with a puzzled expression. 'Pretty, maybe; but not beautiful. Not like you.' She cocked her head and frowned at Madeline's expression. 'My God! You don't even know it, do you?'

Madeline swallowed, blinking, and Becky laughed out loud. And then, as if she'd suddenly remembered that she didn't like Madeline at all, she bent back to her work and said gruffly. 'Now get your breakfast and get out of here. I'm leaving at noon today, and I've got a lot of work to finish before then.'

Madeline hesitated for a moment, then whispered, 'I forgot something upstairs,' and turned to rush down the hall, up the steps, as fast as she could go, as if it would all disappear before she had a chance to see it. She raced into her room and skidded to a halt in front of the mirror, panting, her eyes wide and wondering, her lips parted.

Beautiful? She frowned a little, examining her reflection. She *did* seem to have a little more colour in her face from being outside so much; but, other than that, she looked just as bland as she always had. Light grey eyes; still-light complexion, in spite of the sun; light, light hair, caught now in a crazily tilting ponytail. . .everything about her was so damned light, like an over-exposed photograph. That wasn't beauty. Beauty commanded attention. Anyone knew that. It walked into a room in the form of people like Becky, exuding vitality and colour, and heads turned and everybody noticed.

She sighed, feeling horribly betrayed, as if Becky had handed her a beautifully wrapped present that had turned out to be nothing more than an empty box.

Elias found her in the rose garden an hour later, hunched over a cluster of dried, brittle stems, pulling gummy leaves and grasses away from the seemingly dead plant, carefully cultivating the exposed soil mound with her fingers.

'You're wasting your time.' His voice came from behind without warning, and she jerked her head up and spun on her knees in surprise.

When he saw her face, he smiled quickly, involuntarily, then reached down and brushed a smudge of soil from the tip of her nose. 'Charming,' he said, and suddenly she was embarrassed by the way she looked. Her jeans were damp and black from the knees down, with long streaks of earth across her thighs where she'd wiped her hands. Out of the corner of her eye she could see wisps of hair that had escaped her pony-tail, free-floating in the gentle breeze. She reached up to tuck them behind her ears and stopped at the last moment because her hands were caked with soil. He finished the gesture for her, squatting to his heels close to her, watching his hands as they collected and tamed the vagrant strands.

Madeline watched his face with parted lips threatening a smile, marvelling at how different he looked under the sun, away from the artificial lights of the windowless studio. The green of his eyes matched the burgeoning lilac bushes in the background behind him; his hair quivered in the fickle currents of air, strands of blue glimmering in the black; even his mouth seemed softer, less grim.

'It's dead, you know.' He inclined his head towards the rose plant.

'No,' she murmured, reaching up without thinking, grasping his hand, pulling it down to guide his fingers to the bud graft at the base of the plant, just beneath the soil. 'Feel that? The hard ball on the stem? And then here, gently now. . .that little protrusion? That's the beginning. It's coming to life.' She smiled down at the stiff, dried sticks, enchanted by the imminent miracle of awakening spring. 'Isn't it the most marvellous thing? To feel that happening right beneath your hands?'

When she looked up at his face again, she started at his expression. For a moment, just a moment, his eyes seemed to reflect the feelings of her own heart; a tenderness so deeply felt it was visible in the softness of his gaze. . .but then suddenly his features tightened and he pulled his hand abruptly from hers.

He pushed against his knees and rose as if the moment had never happened, looking around at the dozens of rose mounds she'd cleared already, the short stubs pruned back to the living part of the stems. 'I hadn't noticed how much you'd done out here.'

'I don't know how you could have. You haven't left the studio in days.'

He glanced back at her, and something in his eyes made her look down at where her hands were splayed across her thighs.

'As it happens,' he went on tonelessly, 'I'm leaving the studio today. You can practise in there if you like, or take the afternoon off. I won't be back until evening.'

Inch by inch her shoulders sagged as she watched him walk away, towards the house, towards Becky. They were both gone by the time she came in for lunch.

She stood just inside the kitchen doorway, a little shocked by the intensity of what she was feeling. It wasn't just loneliness, or envy, or jealousy, or even a combination of all of those things. It was deeper than that, and stronger than that—a growing seed of rebellion, not just because she was excluded, but because she wasn't even considered at all. He'd left with Becky without a single qualm about leaving her behind, as if she were some machine that could simply be turned off when it was no longer needed. As far as he was concerned, she wasn't a person at all; just a pair of hands with no function away from a keyboard. The only time he acknowledged her existence was when she performed like a trained animal in the studio, but, dammit, she was more than that. She was a human being, too; a *woman*, just like

Becky. . .and maybe it was high time he noticed.

She spent the better part of the afternoon bathing, washing her hair, performing all those rituals of physical enhancement she had never in her life employed before.

It was near dusk by the time she had finished, and she was glad of that. She liked the way the rose-gold light enhanced the new colour in her face, and she hadn't liked anything about her appearance in so long that her own reflection surprised her.

Her hair was piled softly on top of her head, with a few wisps trailing over her brow and curling at her ears. She'd been lavish with the smoky shadow, and her eyes seemed to smoulder beneath thick lashes darkened with mascara.

The dress was a sleeveless ice-blue silk she'd bought for a student's recital, and worn only that once. At the time it had embarrassed her that the fabric clung to every curve, mocking the modesty of its high mandarin collar, but now she was glad of it.

The skirt was loose enough to wrap provocatively around thigh and hip when she moved, and she tested the effect in front of the mirror, eyes wide and uncertain. She had never been able to define the line that separated sensuality from simple bad taste, but one thing was certain: he wouldn't be able to ignore her dressed like this, if only because she looked so unlike herself.

And if he tries hiding in the studio again tonight, she thought, I'll just wobble out there in these stupid heels and insist that he take me to dinner. This is one night I'm not going to eat alone.

She teetered a little on the unfamiliar spike heels when she heard the slam of the front door.

He was standing at the bottom of the stairs when she descended, just as he had been that first night, almost as if he'd been waiting for her to make just this entrance. She met his eyes boldly as she came down, feeling the swish of silk against her legs, smiling when she heard the quiet hiss of a breath drawn quickly between his teeth.

His eyes touched every part of her body long before she was within range of his hands, then suddenly they fixed on hers with a gaze so cold that it felt like a tangible force threatening to push her backward.

'I'd almost forgotten what day it was,' he said disgustedly, then, without another word, he turned and walked out of sight down the hall, through the kitchen, and out of the back door, slamming it behind him.

Madeline stood paralysed on the stairs, baffled by his reaction, her thoughts repeating over and over that maybe being invisible wasn't so bad. Being seen, and then rejected, was worse. Much worse.

# CHAPTER NINE

MADELINE didn't know how long she'd been standing on the stairs, heart and mind deadened by Elias's cool exit; but she started when there was a sudden light rap on the front door below, and felt a prickling where her hand was gripping the banister, as if that was all that had been holding her up.

She found the presence of mind to call out, 'Come in,' and the silk of her dress rustled against her legs as she shifted her weight.

David walked through the door, looked up at her, then stopped dead. 'Good lord,' he whispered, his eyes racing from the light, fairy-like crown of her hair down to the daring simplicity of her dress. He swallowed once, like a nervous schoolboy, and gazed up at her with a look so unabashedly admiring that Madeline felt the spirits that Elias had crushed lift slightly.

'Thank you, David,' she whispered gratefully, coming down the rest of the stairs. She stood on tiptoe to kiss his cheek, her hands resting lightly on his shoulders, marvelling that she could actually perform such a gesture. It was easy with David. Something about him encouraged the simple, harmless demonstration of affection. 'You will never know how much I needed that.'

His hands fumbled at her waist as she leaned her upper body backwards, bemused by his look of wonder. The expression was as alien to his normally self-assured countenance as his silence was to his nature, and Madeline felt the glow of a compliment that didn't require words.

She smiled up at his brown eyes, the boyish tangle of dark curls clustered on his head. 'You're looking especially handsome tonight yourself,' she told him, patting the cream-coloured lapels of his linen suit. Oddly enough, the ice-blue shirt beneath matched the colour of her dress almost perfectly.

His chest rose with a breath he blew out through his cheeks, and that seemed to restore his power of speech. 'I'm not even going to try to tell you how you look. They haven't invented the right word yet.'

Madeline blushed and dismissed the excessive praise with an embarrassed shrug.

'Shall we go?'

Madeline hesitated, frowning. 'Go where?'

'To dinner, of course. We have reservations at the Hilltop Inn. . .' He stopped and cocked his head at her expression. 'Dinner,' he said carefully. 'You. Me. Friday night. Didn't Elias tell you I was coming?'

She caught her lower lip between her teeth and frowned. 'Actually, what he said was that he told you not to come. . .'

'And because Elias said I shouldn't, you assumed I wouldn't?'

Madeline tried to smile, flustered. 'Actually, David, I meant to call you and tell you to come anyway, but we've just been so busy. . .' She shrugged helplessly, wondering how such a thing had slipped her mind. 'I guess I forgot.'

He hesitated, then spoke very slowly, his eyes roaming with frank puzzlement over her hair, her dress. 'You mean you weren't expecting me?'

She held her breath for a moment, her mind scrambling for an excuse for her appearance, then released it in a feeble laugh. 'Actually, I was just about to take myself out to dinner. I was sick to death of jeans and sweatshirts and being cooped up here. . .' She paused and sighed, looking at him, and added with a sincerity that couldn't be doubted, 'But you have no idea how glad I am to have company. Especially yours.'

He lifted her chin with two fingers, and questioned her gently with his eyes. She dropped hers, rather than answer him, and after a moment his hands fell to his side. 'Where's Elias?' he asked pointedly. 'I should at least say hello before we leave——'

'Can it wait, David?' she blurted out. 'To tell you the truth, I'm starved.' She rushed to the cupboard, snatched a light shawl and her handbag, then turned towards him expectantly. He was just standing there, hands shoved in his trouser pockets, eyeing her curiously.

'Of course it can,' he said quietly. 'As a matter

of fact, I don't really have to see Elias at all.' He held out one hand and smiled at her with an expression that made her think David Whitney was a good deal more perceptive than most people thought. 'Come on, angel. Let me take you away from all this.'

Hilltop Inn was predictably perched on a hill overlooking the small town, just a few miles from Rosewood. It was a casually elegant place of snowy linen and sparkling crystal, saved from pretentiousness by distressed wooden floors and walls of natural brick. The tables were small, intimate worlds of candle-lit isolation, well-separated from one another.

'This is lovely,' Madeline commented as they were seated at a corner table near the fireplace.

'Then it's a perfect background for you.'

It was one of those reflexive compliments people seemed to deliver on cue, and Madeline found herself taking little pleasure from it. 'You always say exactly the right thing, David,' she sighed, shaking her head at him. 'Flattery is your specialty, isn't it?'

He cocked his head, the picture of innocent puzzlement. 'Flattery offends you?'

'No,' she smiled gently. 'Of course not. It's just that I get the feeling you've said the same words before, hundreds of times. You said yourself you were the friendly part of the partnership. It's part of your job, isn't it? Smoothing all the feathers Elias ruffles?'

He was so still that she wondered for a

moment if he was even breathing. His dark eyes never wavered from hers. 'Yes,' he answered finally. 'It *is* part of my job, and that's the rub, isn't it?' His lips curved in a rueful smile, and he signalled for the wine steward. 'No one ever knows when I really mean it.'

Six hours later, well after two in the morning, David's forefinger was pressed crookedly against lips that seemed permanently fixed in a foolish smile. 'Shh,' he hissed dramatically. 'Mus'n' wake the dragon.'

Madeline shook her head in amused exasperation, staggering under the weight of his arm across her shoulders as they stumbled from the car to the house. 'The dragon sleeps in the studio,' she explained for the tenth time, nearly tripping on the raised bricks of the front path.

David, a self-proclaimed disciple of moderate social drinking, had consumed an unbelievable amount of alcohol over the course of the evening. It had started harmlessly enough with a shared half-bottle of wine, but as time wore on he began to drink recklessly, with the dogged determination of a man intentionally bound for inebriation.

And you certainly achieved that, she thought, propping his seemingly boneless form against the wall to the right of the door as she dug in her purse for the house-key. By the time she found it, he was sliding inexorably downwards, and she jumped to catch him under the arms and pull him upright again.

In a disastrously uncoordinated gesture, he tried to fling his arm over her shoulder again, but succeeded only in dislodging her hair from its pins and popping the single button that fastened her dress at the neck. The bodice flap flipped down, and, even though it exposed only her neck, it made her feel vulnerable somehow.

'Oh, terrific,' she muttered as stray strands of blonde hair tumbled from their perch to dangle haphazardly over her face and shoulders. It was the final touch, she was sure, to a state of total dishevelment, but at this point all she cared about was getting them both inside and to bed.

She pushed the door open with one foot, grunted with the effort of literally hauling him inside and repeating the same process all over again. Prop him up against the wall, steady him, flip the entrance light switch, then move quickly to close and lock the door behind them. . .

He'd slid all the way down to the floor this time, and sat with his legs sprawled, his chin on his chest, the foolish smile still in place, even in sleep.

'Oh, David,' she sighed, shaking her head, wondering how on earth she could possibly get him up again.

She turned to put her handbag and shawl on the hall table, then gasped to see Elias leaning silently against the living-room doorway. She took a quick step backwards, her heart thumping with alarm at the start he'd given her.

He just stood there, saying nothing, green eyes empty, his face expressionless. There were deep valleys tracking through his hair, as if he'd run his hands back through it over and over again; a few wilful strands dangled over his forehead like black cuts. He looked down at where David was slumped against the wall, happily oblivious; then back up at her ruined hair and displaced dress.

She touched her hair self-consciously, then the front of her dress. 'David's had a little too much to drink,' she explained hesitantly.

'I can see that.'

She waited for him to say something else, and when the silence became awkward she turned slowly and went to crouch at David's side, smoothing the dark curls back from his forehead. 'Well?' she said over her shoulder, pretending nonchalance. 'Are you going to help me get him upstairs?'

She heard him push away from the wall, walk over to stand next to her; then she saw strong, broad hands reach down. She stood up and moved out of the way, watching as Elias hefted David's dead weight to his chest. He looked down at his friend's head lolling on his shoulder then looked up again and met her eyes. 'Your room or the guest room?' he asked.

'No jokes, please,' she sighed, closing her eyes. 'I'm too tired.'

'What made you think I was joking?'

She opened her eyes and looked at him, trying

to read his expression so she could decide whether to be insulted or not, but his face remained blank. Finally she simply turned away and walked upstairs to the room next to hers.

She flipped on the wall switch, turned back the covers on the bed, then stood aside as Elias laid David down, removed his shoes, jacket and tie, then covered him with surprising gentleness. It was almost like watching a parent tuck a child in for the night.

Finally he stepped back from the bed and straightened, nearly colliding with her. They were shocked to find themselves suddenly so close, and their eyes met briefly, then jerked downwards, afraid to look too long at what they had seen in each other's glance.

Madeline held her breath as her gaze fastened on his right hand, hanging less than an inch from her left, so close that if she moved only slightly their fingers might brush. She lifted her eyes long enough to see that he was watching their hands too, then looked down again expectantly, as if their fingers were actors on a stage, and their next movements would be somehow profound.

His forefinger twitched slightly, almost touched hers, and she caught her breath, waiting, watching, surprised to see her own fingers lift slightly towards his in an automatic response. Suddenly it seemed that their hands were separate entities, playing out a drama that neither could control, and when his fingertips

brushed hers, perhaps accidentally, the impact
was enormous.

Madeline caught her breath in a faint, yet
audible gasp, and out of the corner of her eye
saw his chest hitch abruptly towards hers. A
furtive glance upwards showed the tightness
around his mouth and eyes, the furrows of
confusion on his brow as he watched, apparently helpless to control what his hand was
doing.

Now his fingers were climbing over the top of
her hand, tracing the hollows between the ten-
dons, circling her wrist with a feather-light
pressure that made it strangely hard for her to
breathe. Her lips parted, both in wonder and in
an attempt to draw in more air, as she stared
down, her eyes wide and fixed, fascinated.

When his hand moved up to the soft swell of
her forearm and pressed against it, the intent
was unmistakably erotic, and they both looked
up and their eyes met. His were two spots of
green fire in the dim light of the room, and hers
felt hot and liquid. When her tongue moved
automatically to moisten her lower lip, Elias
frowned hard and made a soft noise deep in his
throat. In the next instant he pulled in an
enormous breath through his teeth and his chest
swelled and brushed against the breasts rising
to meet it, and Madeline almost cried out.

Suddenly David snuffled softly in his sleep
and they both jumped backwards away from
one another. Elias turned his back quickly and

let his head sag on to his shoulders. 'Damn
you,' she heard him exhale hoarsely.

She reached out to touch him, her brows
tipped in puzzlement, but, just before her hand
reached his back, he said, 'Get out of here,' and
she froze, her hand hanging foolishly in mid-
air.

When she didn't move, he turned and
grabbed her hand and almost dragged her into
the hall, then gave her a shove that sent her
stumbling towards her room. She looked back
at him with an expression of complete
bewilderment.

He was staring at her, and a trick of the light
made it look as though the green colour were
spilling from his eyes down the hall towards
her. 'What on earth made you think I'd be
willing to finish what another man started?' he
asked coldly. 'Maybe next time you'll have
enough sense to choose a man who won't pass
out before he can perform.'

Madeline's face went suddenly still, blanching
beneath the faint colour the sun had given her.
'I can't believe you said that,' she whispered,
and then she turned quickly, went into her
room, and closed and bolted the door behind
her. She didn't know how long she'd been
leaning against it, staring blindly into the dark
room, when she felt the vibration of his knuckles
rapping against the wood.

'Madeline.' The door muffled his low whisper. 'Madeline, please. We have to talk. Let me
in.'

Let me in indeed, she smiled bitterly. That's been the problem from the beginning. I let someone in, and I shouldn't have. I let myself feel again, and I shouldn't have.

'Maddie? Maddie! Let me in!'

Without making a sound, her lips formed the ludicrous words of the nursery rhyme—'Not by the hair of my chinny-chin-chin'—and then she buried her face in her hands.

# CHAPTER TEN

IT WAS mid-morning by the time the rumble of muted thunder finally woke Madeline. She lay quietly for a long moment, staring at the ceiling, her mind blank. Finally she sighed, rolled out of bed, padded to the window, and peered out at the gloom of the season's first rainstorm. Everything looked wet and bleak; even the rose garden was mired in mud, and somehow that seemed appropriate.

Slowly, dispiritedly, she began to dress, her emotions so numbed that she didn't even dread facing Elias after last night. What did it really matter if he thought she'd intended to go to bed with David, or even if he thought she was callous enough to accept another man as a substitute at the last minute? That only made her a whore, and, at the moment, being thought of as a whore seemed a whole lot better than being pitied for what she really was: a lonely woman who had grasped desperately at the straws of fantasy, entranced by the delusion that she and Elias were two parts of the same whole, that they were both helpless against the force that drew them together—but that had only been the pathetic imagining of an unloved child who had never quite grown up.

She frowned, concentrating hard on the memories of those scattered moments when she'd felt the electricity between them—when you *thought* you felt the electricity between you, she amended. You wanted that mystical, spiritual bond to exist so badly that you made it up, but it was never there for him. He wanted you here because you were the one person who played his music the way he wanted it to sound. And then you complicated things by wanting more, forcing him to reject you again and again, until the situation became so awkward that even the music went bad. She smiled sadly, because the music was the only thing he'd ever wanted from her, and now she couldn't even give him that.

She scowled and blinked rapidly to hold back the tears as she dressed. She pulled on snug black flannel leggings and a heavy grey sweater that hung to mid-thigh, then brushed out her hair, letting it fall where it would. The grey eyes in the mirror looked strangely lifeless now, and she turned away from them with barely a second glance.

The house itself seemed subdued by the storm; as gloomy and dark as her mood as she made her way downstairs, then towards diffused golden light coming from the kitchen. She reached out to touch things absently as she walked: the antique table in the hall with its empty vase, waiting for the flowers of spring, the gleaming wood of the door-frame that led into the kitchen—little things; things she hadn't known existed just a week ago, but things she would remember for the rest of her life.

Her heart seemed to twist in on itself when she saw Elias sitting at the kitchen table.

He was dressed in black from neck to ankle in a heavy jogging suit, looking every bit as forbidding as the bleak landscape he stared at out of the window, and yet, to Madeline, every bit as promising, too. There was something else beneath the cold, distant façade he wore—she'd sensed it from the beginning—something warm and full of life and infinitely precious. He was like the rose garden in that way, and she wondered if she'd ever see either one of them bloom.

His arms were braced on the table, his hands curled around a steaming mug of coffee. He turned his head sharply when she came in, and a black strand of his hair tumbled to hang over his forehead in a comma.

'Good morning,' she said quietly, moving past the table to where the coffee-maker sat on the work-top. 'Where's Becky?' She felt his eyes on her as she fumbled with the pot.

'It's Saturday. She doesn't come at weekends.'

She risked a glance in his direction, saw that he'd returned his attention to the rivulets of rain running down the window glass, then filled a mug with strong black coffee and leaned back against the work-top.

'I don't suppose David will be up for hours.'

He nodded absently, and she noticed how tired he looked. There were faint smudges under his eyes, he hadn't shaved yet, and his black hair was tousled, as if he hadn't slept very well. She jumped visibly when he turned his head and caught her staring.

'You look tired,' she said quickly, to cover her embarrassment.

'So do you.'

She shrugged and looked down at her coffee, wondering what to say. As it turned out, he spoke first. His voice was stiff and impassive, as if he were reciting a memorised speech.

'I want to talk to you about last night, and about the music—the trouble I've been having composing. It's all connected, you know. I just didn't want to admit it.'

Madeline clutched her mug desperately, staring down into it as if it held the secrets of the universe and she couldn't bring herself to look away. 'I know that,' she mumbled. 'You don't have to say anything. I'm the reason you haven't been able to write.'

He was silent for so long that she finally risked glancing up at him, her lips pressed together in a white line, two spots of embarrassed colour flaming on her cheeks.

His chin dropped into his hand as he turned his head, looking out through the window. 'It was my fault, not yours. I should have seen this coming that first night in your apartment. It was perfectly obvious then that. . .' he paused and frowned, hard '. . .that emotions were going to get in the way of any working relationship between us.'

Madeline closed her eyes briefly, mortified by the memory of how quickly, how eagerly she had agreed to shut down her life and follow him. Even then she must have seemed like a lovesick fan desperate for attention from the object of her adoration.

He pressed his lips together, watching her. 'It was pretending the emotion wasn't there that was causing all the problems, but last night the pretending stopped, didn't it?' He spread his hands and shrugged eloquently. 'I know it doesn't make any sense, but last night. . .having everything out in the open. . .it was like a dam bursting. I couldn't stop writing. I stayed up all night and finished the title song.'

Madeline's face stilled as she struggled to keep it expressionless. Suddenly it didn't matter if all he wanted her for was her playing; it didn't matter if this were just another temporary place where she would leave part of her heart behind; all that mattered was today, and maybe tomorrow; making music together; being close to him for just a little longer.

'We don't have to feel the same way about each other to make great music, Madeline. Even if the music is *all* we ever make together, it's more than most people accomplish in a lifetime.' His eyes were eloquent, deeply green, soft with an emotion she couldn't read.

She swallowed hard, and it took all her courage to keep from bursting into tears. This is what they meant, she thought, when all the old poets talked about unrequited love. This is the agony of sacrificing everything—your life, your pride, the last of your self-esteem—just to be close to the one person you can't live without, even when you know the feeling will never be returned.

They stared at each other in a palpable, quivering silence that seemed to swell by the minute, threatening to fill the room and smother them both, and then suddenly David came bustling into the kitchen, looking more like an innocent young boy out of church than a man who should have been suffering from an outrageous hangover. 'Good morning, good morning, you two!'

Madeline tried for a brave smile and it only quivered a little.

He grinned at her. 'I take it you carried me upstairs on your back last night?'

She shook her head and nodded towards Elias.

David bent from the waist in a mock bow. 'My thanks, old friend. And my apologies to you, angel.' He walked over and dropped to one knee in front of her, his expression comically contrite. 'I behaved abominably last night, and you have every right to be furious with me. . .although I'm not sure I could stand it if you were.' His dark eyes looked up, imploring forgiveness with a clownish glitter, but

Madeline sensed an undercurrent of genuine remorse.

'It's all right, David,' she said quietly, and he popped to his feet, beaming, making her feel foolish for ever thinking he might have been at all serious.

'The truth is,' he confided to Elias over his shoulder, 'she got me drunk and tried to have her way with me. But I resisted, right to the end. You would have been proud.'

Madeline shook her head, quietly exasperated, but Elias raised one dark brow and spoke very seriously indeed. 'The real truth is that, in all our years together, I've never seen you drunk before.' He hesitated, looking David right in the eye. 'Why last night?'

David's grin froze momentarily, then he covered his hesitation with a nervous laugh and a self-deprecating shrug. 'There's a first time for everything, I guess.' He clapped his hands suddenly, making Madeline jump. 'Now, who wants positively the best omelette they've ever eaten in their life?' He crossed to the refrigerator in two long strides, then dived into the lighted depths to dig through its contents. 'Get some plates, angel, will you? We've all got business to discuss, and business always goes down better with good food.'

He chattered constantly while he cooked, covering a stream of subjects that ran together in confusion, asking questions, then answering them himself, apparently oblivious to the silence of his companions.

It was only when they were all seated around the table, David at the head, Madeline and Elias on opposite sides, that his tone and manner became suddenly businesslike.

'Well, children,' he said sombrely, piercing his omelette with his fork, then examining the bite he selected before tucking it into his mouth. 'Are you both ready to be stars?'

Madeline and Elias glanced briefly at each other, then turned identically expressionless faces to stare at David. 'What are you talking about?' Elias asked.

David grinned and waggled his brows. 'A great promotional gimmick that's going to make us all a fortune, that's what.' He rolled his eyes at Elias's expression of distaste. 'Oh, I know you don't give a damn about the money, Elias, but not everyone at this table has your bank account. Besides, the better the promotion for this movie and its soundtrack, the more albums we'll sell, and the more albums we sell, the more people hear your music, and that's what it's all about for you, isn't it?'

Elias conceded the point with a reluctant shrug. 'So what's all the nonsense about Madeline's and my being stars? We're going to record the music for this movie, not appear in it.'

'Maybe not,' David smiled triumphantly, 'but you sure are going to represent it. I told the producer about angel here,' he winked broadly at Madeline, 'and he wants you both to pose for the album cover. Can't you see it? The Press will have a field day. Art imitates life, all that sort of stuff. By the time this is all over, you two are going to be the hottest romantic couple since. . .' He caught a glimpse of Madeline's blank expression and stopped. 'What's the matter, angel?'

She sat perfectly still, her eyes fixed on David's face. 'What do you mean, "art imitating life"?' she asked in a small voice.

He shrugged, then smiled sheepishly. 'I didn't mean it *was*, of course; just that everyone would *think* it was.' He kept smiling at her for a moment, then faltered at the utter lack of comprehension in her expression. 'The *movie*, Madeline. The plot. Temperamental composer in a tempestuous love affair with his pianist. . .' The look on her face stopped him in mid-sentence. 'You didn't know what the movie was about?'

Madeline shook her head, numbed by the perverse, twisted coincidence. This wasn't art imitating life; it was art mocking her deepest, most secret fantasies. 'I couldn't do that,' she whispered rapidly. Out of the corner of her eye she saw Elias jerk his head to look out of the window, jaw muscles clenched.

'Don't be silly. It's just a photo, just showbiz, and let's not forget, it's going to make you a pile of money. With an advertising gimmick like this, the royalties on the album should be outstanding.'

She took a deep breath and tried to smile, but failed miserably. There was no way she could make David understand, not without saying it outright. How could he know that the only thing she wanted out of life was to have Elias love her? That watching Elias pretend to love her for the camera, knowing it was only a pretence, would be more than she could bear? She looked down at where her hands were twisting nervously in her lap and tried to gather her strength. She had to give them another reason; something that would make sense.

When she finally looked up again, her face was composed, her smile cool. 'If it's really just showbiz, David, there's no reason for me to be on the cover. You could hire someone else; someone more. . .appropriate. A model, maybe.'

'Nope.' David shook his head firmly. 'The real-life composer and his real-life pianist— that's what's going to sell this thing. Besides, we've already got the photo session scheduled, and I promised the producer you'd both be willing participants. Hell, I'm the one who sold him on the idea, angel.'

Madeline felt as if her insides were shrivelling away from her skin; that in just a few moments there would be no substance left; just an empty shell. 'Well, you shouldn't have done that,' she snapped.

Elias jerked his head to glare at her and she paled under his cold green stare. When she looked for comfort in David's face, she saw only impatience, and perhaps a hint of irritation.

'It's just a picture, Madeline,' he said sharply. 'It doesn't mean a thing. You two don't even have to *like* each other. . .' He hesitated, his eyes shifting from one to the other.

'She's right,' Elias broke in suddenly, his voice sounding like a metal hammerhead striking cold steel. 'We can use a model. The public won't know the difference.'

Madeline nodded, pathetically eager. 'I'm not very photogenic anyway, and you could find someone who really *looked* the part. . .' Suddenly her gaze sharpened and she looked directly at Elias. 'Like Becky.'

Elias stared at her, saying nothing, and finally David prompted, 'Becky? You're kidding.'

'You know Becky?' Madeline asked.

'Well of course I know *of* her. . . Elias talks about her all the time. . .' Madeline winced a little at that '. . .but we've never actually met, and I sure as hell would never have thought of using her for this——'

'Why not?' Madeline interrupted, pushing back the pain. 'She'd be perfect. She's one of the most beautiful women I've even seen. The producer will love having her photo on the album cover, and I bet Becky would love to do it.' She felt the chill of Elias's gaze, but when she looked at him, he just shrugged.

'She probably *would* love it,' he told David. 'And what's the difference who poses for the cover, as long as the public buys the concept?'

David's frown was troubled, but after he'd assessed the tension between Elias and Madeline, he sighed with resignation. 'Well, if you both agree it's worth considering, we'll consider it.' He shrugged once, as if the decision were inconsequential.

'Come on,' Elias said, getting up abruptly. 'I'll follow you as far as the village. We'll stop at Becky's and you can meet her yourself.'

David rose, dark eyes sparkling with mischief. 'Beautiful, eh?' he said, rubbing his hands together in a pretence of lasciviousness, but Elias's response made him take a quick step backwards, startled.

'Don't even think about her that way, David,' he said, his eyes glinting with fierce protective-ness. 'Becky is off-limits to that sort of thing.'

David raised one brow, genuinely offended. 'I know that, Elias,' he said softly. 'I've always known that.'

Madeline closed her eyes and looked away. It shouldn't have hurt so much just to hear Elias finally say aloud what she had known all along, but somehow it did.

'Hey, angel.' David was standing next to her chair, smiling down at her with an expression she couldn't quite read. He reached out and cupped her chin gently in his palm. 'Call me. Any time.' His eyes shifted to look at Elias, hardening slightly. 'You don't mind Madeline calling me, do you, Elias?'

He touched her briefly with his eyes, and his gaze chilled her. 'She can do whatever she wants. Now let's get the hell out of here.'

Madeline remained at the table, motionless, long after she had heard the two cars start and pull out of the drive.

If I had a friend, she thought sadly, I'd call them now, and we'd talk and laugh and maybe cry a little, and then I'd feel better.

After a time she rose from the kitchen chair like an old woman, and walked woodenly through the house to the parlour. There she sat in front of the only friend she'd ever had, placed her hands on the keyboard, and began to talk.

Outside the rain continued to fall.

# CHAPTER ELEVEN

MADELINE spent the next week trying to slip back into the private world that had been her sanctuary before Elias came into her life. It was a safe, comfortable place that admitted no one, and the truth was that over the years she had learned to function very well there, secure behind the impenetrable walls of indifference. But finding that sanctuary again was harder than she had ever thought possible.

I'm just his employee, a hired pianist who happens to live in, she kept telling herself; but simply being in the same room with him was almost exquisitely painful. Knowing he could never feel the same way about her had not dulled the iridescent green of his eyes or lessened the impact of his presence, and she still couldn't stop her heart from lurching whenever he walked into a room, his dark brows lowered in a scowl, jaw clenched in a silent, inexplicable rage that had been constant since she'd balked at posing for the album cover.

Shutting out the rest of the world was a lot easier than shutting out Elias. During the past week, Becky had faded into a shadowy, silent ghost who was always there when she woke up, always gone by evening. Like Elias, she too had become more hostile, but if Madeline noticed at all it was in the way of noticing the angry buzzing a fly you simply brushed aside. You didn't stop to analyse why the fly was agitated; you just shrugged it away.

Even the advancement of spring, with all its raucous, happy-drunk noise and colour, barely penetrated Madeline's senses, and the joy she had once found in the rose garden was gone. She still gardened every morning while Elias worked in the studio, but she no longer felt that old rush of elation to find a plant stirring to life beneath her hands. It had been replaced with an almost obsessive sense of purpose, as if bringing the garden to life were a joyless, tedious task, but one that had to be accomplished for a reason she couldn't quite remember.

The one thing that still touched her, that constantly threatened the chilly barriers she was erecting, was the new music Elias was writing. It was unmistakably his music—still clean and bright and shockingly intense—but, in a way she couldn't pinpoint, it was vastly different than anything he had written before. For the first time she didn't feel that the music spoke directly to her, that she alone could feel the touch of his troubled spirit and translate it for the world. Her heart still soared and plummeted as she played, but now the music seemed to speak to a greater audience, an audience so vast she felt lost in its numbers.

By Wednesday she'd realised what Elias had

yet to see—that this new music was not theirs
alone, that its voice belonged to everyone. In it
you could hear the cries of joy of anyone who
had ever loved, the heart-rending pain of
anyone who had ever loved and lost. It was the
kind of music that could play to an audience of
thousands and strike an identical chord in each
heart, because it was the song of human experi-
ence common to all men.

On Friday morning she stood in front of the
dressing-table mirror in the little bedroom she'd
come to think of as hers, staring thoughtfully at
her reflection. In a way, she had been transformed in the short time she had been here. Her
body seemed to glow with new strength, nur-
tured by fresh air and tightened by exercise, and
there was a definite aura of health and fitness
where once there had only been pallor and
malaise. The sun had given new colour to her
face while it had taken colour from her hair, in a
clean demonstration of nature's continuous
trade-offs. Only her eyes remained
unchanged—still the arctic grey they had always
been, once again empty of dreams.

She brushed her hair carefully until it swept
over her shoulders in a smooth wave, and, on
impulse, put on a rose-coloured cotton sundress
with funny spaghetti straps that left her neck
and shoulders bare. It was the kind of dress she
imagined a farmer's daughter would wear; the
kind of campy thing New York women liked to
wear for Sunday afternoon picnics in Central

Park, because it completed their false, temporal image of country living. It was a totally impractical outfit for working in the rose garden, but she wouldn't be doing that today anyway.

After a few deep breaths she placed her hairbrush very carefully back on the dressing-table, then went downstairs.

In the kitchen, Becky glanced up from what she was stirring on the stove with an expression of obvious dislike. 'Doesn't look much like a gardening outfit.' She nodded at the pink sundress.

Madeline's smile was thin as she looked at Becky, really seeing her for perhaps the first time this week. It was no wonder Elias loved her. The faded jeans and denim work-shirt did nothing to detract from the strength and beauty of the body beneath, and even without make-up her dark eyes crackled with a lovely, fierce intensity. Her hair was pulled away from her face, a few damp tendrils escaping to dangle at her ears. 'You and Elias are going to look perfect together on that album cover,' she murmured.

Becky's eyes flashed angrily at her. 'Yes, you managed to arrange that very nicely, didn't you?' she said snidely. 'It wouldn't have cost you a damn thing to pose for that stupid cover, but you couldn't be bothered to even do that much.'

Madeline's jaw dropped open and she blinked stupidly, wondering why on earth Becky was so angry. By all rights she should have been thrilled by the chance to pose with the man she loved for a photo that would be seen all over the world. 'I thought you'd be happy to do it, Becky,' she said, mystified.

'I *am* happy to do it!' she snapped. 'I'd do anything for Elias.'

'Well, then.' Madeline frowned uncertainly. 'It really won't make a bit of difference who poses with him. As long as the public thinks you're his pianist, it won't affect the cover's impact, or the number of sales. . .'

Becky's smile was almost frightening, it was so cold. 'No,' she said quietly. 'I suppose it won't make a bit of difference.' She snatched her spoon up from the stove top and began stirring furiously at whatever was in the pot. 'Don't forget you're going along to the photo session tomorrow. David says the producer wants to hear the theme song, and you'll have to play it.'

Madeline felt her heart slip from her chest to her stomach in a nauseating slide. 'No one told me I was supposed to go along,' she whispered numbly.

Becky glanced up, some of the anger leaving her face when she saw Madeline's dismayed expression. 'Don't tell me you're nervous about playing for the producer?'

Madeline's mouth twitched in an empty smile. 'No, of course not.' She looked around the room vacantly, telling herself she would deal with tomorrow when it arrived. It wouldn't be so bad, playing Elias's music for a room full of people. . .laying open her soul to anyone who cared to listen. . . After a long moment her eyes closed and she lifted her hand to press two fingers into the space between her brows, as if to push back inside thoughts that should never be spoken aloud. Her voice was calm by the time she looked at Becky again. 'I thought I'd drive into the village today. Do you think Elias would let me use the car?'

Becky shrugged. 'I can pick up whatever you need and bring it back on Monday. What do you want?'

Madeline looked down at the floor, her lower lip caught between her teeth. 'Actually. . . I was thinking of getting some house paint. . .'

The spoon Becky was holding clattered against the side of the pot, and she turned slowly to look at Madeline. 'You want to paint the house?'

Madeline hesitated, then nodded. 'Just the shutters, maybe the window trim. . .'

Becky's eyes narrowed. 'Why on earth would you want to do that?'

Madeline looked away. Why, indeed? How could she explain such a thing to a woman like Becky, a woman who had always had a home, a place where she belonged?

Just once, Madeline wanted to leave her mark on a place she loved before she was forced to leave; to change the place as places had always changed her; to leave a piece of herself behind that would say Madeline Chambers had been here; Madeline Chambers had made a difference. 'It needs doing,' she said simply, knowing Becky would never understand the real reason. 'Most of the wood is bare. It'll rot if it doesn't get some protection for the weather soon.'

'Why should you care what happens to this house?'

Madeline's faint brow twitched. 'It's a wonderful house,' she replied, somehow sensing that if she didn't come to the house's defence, no one would.

'Well, you'd better ask Elias before you do anything,' Becky snapped irritably, turning back to the stove.

'I'll do that,' Madeline said, crossing the kitchen towards the back door without so much as getting a cup of coffee.

The rose garden seemed to reproach her for her neglect as she walked quickly through the now neatly tended mounds on her way to the studio. The earthy smell of newly turned soil assailed her nostrils, following her through the white pines and on to the path across the grassland. I'll miss that, she thought with a regretful smile. When the inevitable happens, when I finally have to leave this place, I'll miss a lot of things, but perhaps most of all I'll miss the smell of the earth itself.

She hesitated at the heavy door of the studio,

took a deep breath, then pulled it open on its silent hinges.

Elias hadn't heard her come in. He was too engrossed in whatever melody he was picking out on the keyboard with one hand. His other cradled his chin, elbow propped on the music ledge.

Madeline had never caught him unaware before; had never once seen him when he didn't know she was looking, and a surge of unexpected tenderness washed over her at the sight.

He wore a short white terry robe, his legs and feet were bare, and his hair was a boyish tangle of dark wetness that curled at his forehead and the nape of his neck. Most startling of all was the way he was smiling wistfully as he plunked at a melody her brain finally registered as 'Chopsticks'.

Madeline thought that perhaps this was the moment she would carry with her for the rest of her life; the single memory of Elias Shepherd she would never be able to erase.

'I think that particular piece has been done before,' she said quietly.

His head jerked around at the sound of her voice, and she saw the intense veneer of the Elias Shepherd she had known for weeks slam down quickly over the one she had just seen for the first time. His eyes seemed to falter a bit at the silly pink sundress, and Madeline thought she probably looked as out of character as he did.

'I've never seen you wear that,' he said.

'I've never seen you wear *that*,' she smiled at his terry robe, and astoundingly he smiled back, and the smile made him look boyish again.

'I just got out of the shower.' He looked down at the keyboard and shook his head with mild exasperation. 'For some reason I haven't been able to get this stupid song out of my head this morning. Must be the first piano ditty every kid ever learns. Remember it?' He punched delicately at the first few bars of the most familiar piano exercise in the world.

Her mind played the bass part as he continued to play the treble, and then suddenly just playing the accompaniment in her mind wasn't enough. 'Chopsticks' wasn't 'Chopsticks' with only two hands on the keys. You just had to have four.

She didn't remember actually crossing the room, sliding next to him on the piano bench, hesitating only a moment before her hands picked up the bass. All she knew was that suddenly they were side by side, both grinning down at the keyboard while the raucous sound of a counterpoint 'Chopsticks' rose from the concert grand with the sound of a syncopated symphony.

They embellished, they ad-libbed, they inserted trills and arpeggios in totally inappropriate places, never thinking how odd it was that the world's most serious composer and the world's most serious pianist were accomplishing together what neither of them had ever accomplished alone: they were having fun with music.

Finally, as if the ending had been carefully prearranged, they both struck a last triumphant chord then grinned sideways at each other over the keyboard, holding each other's eyes for a moment longer than was comfortable.

Disconcerted, Madeline dragged her gaze from his to scowl down at their four hands resting on the keys. At first the silence was awkward, but within seconds it became unbearable. 'I want to paint the shutters,' she blurted out abruptly.

His hands flinched on the keys. 'What?'

Madeline pressed her lips together, her face reddening. 'The shutters,' she began to babble uncontrollably. 'I want to paint the shutters on the house because they're chipped and bare in a lot of places and the wood is going to rot if somebody doesn't take care of it soon and——'

'Maddie.'

She closed her mouth and her eyes abruptly and took a deep breath. 'What?' She couldn't bring herself to look at him.

'I didn't bring you up here to paint that damn house. I don't want the shutters painted. Let them rot.'

Her hair flew as she spun her head to face him, pale eyes snapping open with frustration. She had to concentrate to keep her voice steady. 'What *is* it with you and that house?'

'I hate that house,' he said flatly.

Madeline pursed her lips and frowned. 'That's crazy. Hating a building is crazy.' She hesitated a moment, her own words giving her pause. Was his hating the house any stranger than her loving it? 'You don't know how lucky you were, having a place like that,' she rambled on nervously. 'If you'd never had a home, if you'd never had a place that was always there, you'd understand just how lucky. . .' She stopped at the bright surge of disbelieving curiosity that suddenly brought his eyes to life.

'You've never had a home?' he asked quickly, his hand reaching tentatively for hers.

She jerked her hands down to her lap and stared at them, pursing her lips furiously. 'I had a lot of homes,' she mumbled.

'Your family moved around a lot?'

She shook her head, scowling now, but refused to look at him. 'I don't have a family. I spent my childhood in foster homes—a lot of them. . .'

She could hear the steady sound of his breathing in the silence that followed, and finally raised her eyes tentatively to find him staring at her.

'Paint the shutters, Maddie,' he said quietly. 'Paint the whole damn house if you want.'

# CHAPTER TWELVE

WIVES did this sort of thing, Madeline mused as she strolled the streets of Brighton Square, shopping for paint for Elias's house. The thought, dangerously close to fantasy, lightened her heart. She stopped to peer into shop windows, she smiled and nodded at all the people she met, and, for a time at least, she felt that she belonged in this town, and that this town belonged to her. For this one afternoon, normally sombre and reclusive Madeline Chambers—a woman who dreaded the sidelong glances of strangers who marvelled at her odd pale appearance—had disappeared. There was no trace of that colourless creature in the reflection she saw in shop windows. Instead, there was a sun-kissed, smiling young woman, almost frivolous in a bright rose sundress that echoed the colour of her cheeks—a woman Madeline thought she might like.

By the time she'd returned to Rosewood, Becky had gone home, Elias was sequestered in his studio, and the house and the grounds were hers alone. She exchanged the sundress for baggy jeans and an old T-shirt and went downstairs to paint.

The faded, chipped green of the shutters

surrounded the front windows, making them appear small and sleepy. Instinctively Madeline had decided against a matching green paint, choosing a brilliant white instead. Foolishly, childlishly, she talked to the house as she dipped her brush and touched it to the first shutter. 'This will wake you up; see if it doesn't,' she muttered under her breath, her brush busy. 'You won't look empty and abandoned and closed up any more. You'll be different; you'll be changed, and all because I was here.' She worked diligently, carefully, lovingly; transforming the house as surely as she had transformed the rose garden.

By the time she'd finished the shutters on the front the tan of her arms and face was spattered with white, strands of sweat-dampened hair dangled crazily down her forehead, and the sun had crept to its afternoon home in the western sky. Dripping brush clutched in one hand, she backed up and cocked her head at the house, assessing her work, smiling at what she saw.

Sunlight glanced off the windows that now appeared huge, flinging white arms wide as if to welcome the world. The once-dull bricks seemed warm with a rosy glow, as if the house itself were blushing, a little embarrassed by a rather daring new suit of clothes.

It's perfect, Madeline thought, stretching to ease the nagging ache of her shoulder muscles as her eyes roamed happily over the house. Just perfect. . .except that now the tangle of neglected shrubbery hugging the porch and the path-way looked more unkempt than ever.

Without a second thought, she set aside her painting paraphernalia and plunged headlong into the jungle of untended foliage. By the time she was finished her hands were black with encrusted soil and the muscles in her back and arms were screaming in complaint, but one look at the front of the house made it all worth it. Shapely honeysuckle and blooming dogwood shrubs graced the entrance, with frivolous clusters of fragrant lily of the valley dotting the mulch at their base. Sighing, her hands pressed to the ache in the small of her back, Madeline backed away once again, brushing her soiled hands on the sides of her jeans.

*Now* it's perfect, she thought and then her feet nearly left the ground as Elias spoke from behind her.

'My God, Maddie.' He moved up to stand beside her, his eyes fixed in wonderment on the front of the house. 'First my music, then the rose garden, and now this. . . It seems that everything you touch comes to life.'

Madeline felt her heart leap momentarily, and then still in her chest. Except you, she thought sadly. I can't bring you to life. Only Becky can do that.

She glanced back at the house. 'I love this place,' she murmured.

'You and my mother,' he chuckled sadly. 'She thought the sun rose and set on this little piece of ground.' He looked at her suddenly, frowning a little. 'What made you love the house so much, Maddie?'

Madeline looked down at the ground, lips pressed together. 'When I was a kid,' she began softly, 'I used to dream of having a house of my own. . .a house I'd never have to leave.' She looked back up at the house and took a deep breath. 'It looked just like this one does.'

Elias was silent for a moment, but she could feel his eyes on her. 'You said you had a foster family——'

'I said I had a lot of them,' she corrected him automatically. 'I was never in one place for very long.'

He fell silent again, perhaps imagining a childhood where no one, and no place, was permanent.

The silence made her nervous. It meant he was thinking about what she'd said; probably pitying her, and she didn't want that. 'I told you why I loved the house,' she said suddenly, turning to him with an overly bright smile. 'It's only fair that you tell me why you hate it.'

His features froze, and the green of his eyes seemed to darken as she watched. His smile was thin, laced with bitterness. 'I was happy here as a child, living with my mother, so I thought I would always be happy here, as if happiness were a place, and not a condition.'

He paused and his jaw tightened. Madeline thought his eyes looked like two flat green stones. 'So I brought my wife here to live, after we were married. She hated the place; hated the isolation; and eventually she ended up hating me for bringing her here. I found her in bed with a man I'd thought was my friend—in the very bed you sleep in, as a matter of fact. That was the last day I set foot in this house—until you came.'

Madeline felt his pain like a blow to her stomach, and the feeling was achingly familiar. She knew what it was like to give your heart, then suffer the silent blow of someone who didn't want it giving it back. She'd felt it a dozen times, every time she'd left another foster home.

She looked at the rigid lines of his profile, the defensive set of his jaw, and in his face she saw the child she must have been; the child who struggled so hard to be brave; to pretend that rejection didn't hurt.

The need to comfort was so strong it was almost an ache. She wanted to reach up and press her hand against his cheek, to ease the common pain that had bound her to him from the first time she'd heard echoes of her own despair in his music. She wanted to reach out, but the space between her and another human being was far too vast. Her hand quivered at her side, then stilled. 'I'm sorry,' she murmured.

Elias took her shoulders and turned her gently to face him. 'Sorry?' he asked incredulously. 'My God, Maddie, why should you be sorry? Look what you've done. You've made me see it the way it was when my mother was alive, when the house was filled with love. You've made me realise what a fool I've been, letting one bad memory ruin years of the good ones I had in this place.' He bent forward to press his lips against her forehead. 'Thank you for that, Maddie,' he whispered.

She dropped her head and stared at the paint-spattered toes of her tennis shoes. 'All I did was paint the shutters,' she mumbled, embarrassed.

Elias gazed tenderly at the top of her bent head. When he finally spoke, his voice was a whisper. 'You have no idea what you are, do you, Maddie?'

Madeline raised her eyes quickly to meet his; almost flinched at the depth of the emotion she saw shining there. Oh, no, she begged silently as his face descended towards hers. Oh, no, please don't do that, please don't kiss me, please don't be nice, don't even talk to me, because then I'll want it forever, and nothing is forever, and it hurts so much to keep learning that lesson again and again. . .

His lips were the merest brush of a butterfly wing, and then he was at a safe distance again, smiling down at her. There. That wasn't so frightening. It hadn't been a man-to-woman kiss after all; more like the tender, gentle kiss of a father, or a brother, or a friend whose heart is filled with gratitude. There had been no passion in it. None at all. Madeline blinked rapidly to hold back the same tears she'd been holding back for most of her life.

'We were supposed to be friends, remember?' he asked quietly.

Madeline nodded, not trusting her voice.

'So can two friends go out to dinner together?'

Her lips quivered with the beginnings of a smile.

'We'll celebrate. The music, the house. . .' his eyes fixed on hers '. . .friendship.'

Madeline showered and dressed hurriedly in a simple, conservative dress of navy blue linen— the kind of dress one would wear to a dinner with friends. There was nothing seductive about the modest square neckline with its white trim, nothing suggestive in the way the fabric fell in a straight line from shoulder to hem, and that was good. She couldn't allow herself to think of this dinner as anything more than an interlude with a friend.

She brushed her hair almost carelessly, letting it crackle over her shoulders in a silvery mist, then frowned curiously at her reflection. Her eyes looked different, as if there were a hint of green beneath the arctic grey. For one fanciful moment she wondered if even the wintriest heart held the promise of spring, trying to break through the icy shield of pretended indifference. If eyes are truly the windows to the soul, she thought, then mine are revealing too much. She scowled at her reflection, then turned quickly from the mirror.

She'd expected to find Elias at the bottom of the stairs or, failing that, in the kitchen, the only other place in the house he seemed comfortable. It surprised her to finally find him waiting for her in the small parlour, perfectly at ease in a wing chair with his feet propped up on an ottoman.

'There you are.'

He looked up at her and smiled. 'Should I have left a trail of breadcrumbs?'

She chuckled out loud, then started at the sound. How long had it been since she'd heard herself laugh? 'I've just never seen you in here before, that's all.'

He glanced over at the baby grand piano in the corner, his eyes distant for a moment. 'I had my first piano lesson in this room, on that very piano. I was awful. My mother was the real pianist in the family.'

Madeline walked over to the wall of photos and looked at one in particular; one of a young, gangly boy with an impish grin and dark hair falling over his forehead. She looked over her shoulder at him. 'Is this you?'

He nodded. 'The one next to it is of my mother.'

A young woman smiled at Madeline from the photo. She stood in the middle of the rose garden, surrounded by blooms. 'She looks a little like you in that photo,' Elias said from across the room.

'No, she doesn't. She's beautiful.'

'So are you, Madeline. Don't you know that?'

The room was so silent she thought she could hear the sound of her heartbeat.

He sighed and cleared his throat. 'I'm starved; how about you?'

She turned with a smile that faltered a bit when she saw him rise from his chair, and wondered if the day would ever come when the simple sight of this man failed to move her. He was wearing trim, dark trousers and a white shirt that billowed away from his body with every movement. The contrast between his black hair and light skin seemed more pronounced now, as if she'd drawn her own new colour of health more from him than the sun. 'I'm ready.' And she nodded, walking over to take his offered arm.

It felt right to Madeline, walking through the house they both loved arm-in-arm. . .too right; too perfect. She caught her lower lip between her teeth as they walked out of the house, towards the car. She knew what happened when things were too perfect.

They ended.

# CHAPTER THIRTEEN

MADELINE and Elias ate supper at a crowded little Italian café tucked out of sight on one of the village's back-streets. 'It's not in the guidebooks,' Elias told her on the way in, 'but travellers seem to find it anyway. I think you'll like it.'

Like so many of the great Italian eateries of the east, there were no pretensions here. No candles stuck in Chianti bottles, no red-checked tableclothes, no garish wall murals or straining violins. The interior of the place was almost spartan, with simple wooden tables and chairs, dark panelling, and dim lights. The only concession to atmosphere was a single candle on each table, held by its own drippings to a plain white plate.

'They aren't much on ambience here.' Elias stated the obvious as he guided her past groups of diners to an empty table in the back.

Madeline breathed in the mouthwatering redolence of fresh garlic and spices. 'I'm inhaling the ambience,' she replied, and he rewarded her with one of his rare smiles.

Within the first five minutes what seemed like the entire staff—clearly all members of the same family—had come to the table to greet Elias like a long-lost son or brother. It surprised Madeline a little to see this reserved, contained man as the object of such demonstrative affection. What surprised her more, and charmed her as well, was that their obvious fondness for Elias spilled over to include her, simply because she was with him. She sat blushing at the table after they'd finally been left alone, a little over-whelmed by the unaccustomed attention, the noisy kisses of strangers still burning on her cheeks.

'Sorry about that,' Elias said sheepishly, noting her discomfort. 'The Scarpellos are like family. They're very. . .affectionate.'

Madeline smiled tentatively, remembering the large man with the brilliantly white smile beaming down at her, saying, 'I approve, Elias. She's obviously not Italian, which is unfortunate, but, nevertheless, I approve.'

'They're wonderful,' she murmured, still basking in the warm glow of such immediate acceptance, even though she hadn't known how to respond. Elias focused green eyes on hers with something like surprise. Later she ordered in flawless Italian, setting off a round of noisy, delighted accolades from the Scarpellos, leaving Elias looking more surprised than ever.

'I didn't know you spoke Italian.'

'I speak Italian *food*,' she corrected him. 'That's all.'

Giorgio, the large man who had won her heart with his approval, brought a carafe of deep red

burgundy to the table and presented it with a
flourish, saying, 'From my own cellar. I must
have known you were coming, Elias. I decanted
this earlier.' He beamed at Madeline, passing
her a nearly full glass. 'Drink,' he commanded.
'All great nights of love begin with wine.'

Madeline blushed scarlet.

'She's my pianist, Giorgio,' Elias put in has-
tily, 'not my lover.'

'Simply a matter of time,' Giorgio proclaimed
certainly as he bustled away to cater to other
customers.

Equally uncomfortable, Elias and Madeline
both pretended to gaze nonchalantly at their
surroundings, then their eyes met as though
they were two startled birds, each surprised by
the other. Elias relieved the awkwardness with
a smiling, helpless sigh. 'He's incorrigible. A
die-hard romantic.'

Madeline smiled and felt her shoulder
muscles relax. 'Is he always like this?'

Elias shrugged. 'I've never been here with a
woman before.'

Madeline sipped at her wine, her thoughts
busy with the curiosity of why he and Becky
never ate here together.

When she met his eyes again he was smiling
at her, a little sadly, she thought. The candle-
light flickered in his eyes like yellow spots of
heat centred in cool green glades.

'We never talk, you know,' he said, 'except
about the music. Sometimes, when I listen to

you play what I write, I think you must know more about me than anyone else in the world. . .' Madeline's brows shot up at that '. . .but I don't really know anything about you. I didn't know until this morning that you'd never had a family.'

Madeline's shoulders moved in a nervous shrug. 'It isn't exactly the kind of thing you mention in passing.'

His eyes were unrelenting, almost intrusive. 'You said you had a lot of homes. . .'

'Yes.'

'Do you keep in touch with the families? Are you close to them?'

Her smile flashed automatically, but it was cold, artificial. 'Actually, I was never in one home long enough to get close to anyone.' He looked so stricken that she added defensively, 'Don't look at me like that. Don't feel sorry for me. I have a good life now.'

'I'm not feeling sorry for who you are now, Maddie,' he said softly. 'I'm feeling sorry for the child you were. . .the child who's still inside you, falling in love with houses because she's afraid to fall in love with people.'

Madeline caught her breath, then looked down, blinking rapidly. He knew too much; he *saw* too much. 'You should talk,' she snapped without looking at him. 'You hate houses for the same reason.'

To her surprise he chuckled softly, and she looked up to find him smiling at her again.

'Maybe that's our problem, Maddie. Maybe we're too close, too much alike, in too many ways.' His eyes darkened abruptly and he looked down. 'So tell me. How are things going with you and David?'

Madeline was taken aback by the abrupt change of subject. 'David? I haven't talked to David since he was here, that morning after. . .'

He turned his head to one side and grimaced. 'The morning after I made a total ass of myself,' he finished the sentence in a grumble. 'I'm surprised you'll talk to me at all, after the stupid things I said that night in David's room. There's no excuse for behaving the way I did, except that——' He pressed his lips together, cutting the sentence short. 'Whatever your relationship with David, it's none of my business.'

'I don't have a relationship with David.'

He stared at her silently for a moment, his face expressionless. 'He and I talked that day on the way to Becky's. I think he's in love with you,' he said quietly.

Her smile was sudden and poignant. For just a moment, she allowed herself to imagine what it would be like to be loved by anyone on a long-term basis, but common sense brought the fantasy to an abrupt halt.

'David's the kind of man who loves everyone,' she said, unaware that she was still smiling, that Elias was watching her face intently. 'It's like breathing for him.'

'Maybe. But this is different. Even I can see it.'

Madeline shifted uncomfortably in her seat. The notion of any man falling in love with her was so alien, so preposterous, that it embarrassed her to even hear it spoken aloud. 'Do you mind if we don't talk about David?' she asked with a stiff smile, and his brows lifted.

'Of course,' he replied, his voice suddenly chilly. 'I didn't mean to pry.' He finished his own wine in a single swallow, then refilled both their glasses.

Dinner passed in relative silence, partly because the mention of David had somehow erected an invisible barrier between them, partly because Giorgio was so attentive that they had little time alone. 'Come back,' he told her as they left, flashing his white smile, kissing her noisily on each cheek. 'You're family now.'

In a spontaneous gesture that was totally out of character, Madeline threw her arms around the portly man's neck and pressed her lips together so she wouldn't cry. No one had ever told her she was family before.

On the way back to Rosewood Madeline sat a little sideways in the passenger seat of the car, just enough to be able to see Elias by moving only her eyes.

He'd been right, of course. Inside she was still that little girl, desperately searching for a family, and, for tonight at least, Giorgio had given her the illusion of having one. That sense of belonging surrounded her now, like a warm, comforting blanket, making her feel safe. With the security of family behind you, she thought—even if it is only an illusion—the risks of life seemed suddenly less frightening. She wondered if having a family made everyone feel that way.

'You're smiling.'

She felt his glance just before he looked back at the dark road. 'Am I?'

'You are. Does Italian food always affect you this way?'

'Only Giorgio's,' she said, feeling her smile broaden.

'Then we'll have to go there often.'

It was the kind of thing people said automatically, like, 'I'll call you,' or 'Let's have lunch some time,'; but Madeline didn't care. To her the words had sounded like a promise for the future, and if he hadn't really meant them that way, well, she'd just pretend that he had. She'd been pretending for most of the day already, after all—pretending the town was hers when she'd shopped for paint; pretending Giorgio had really meant it when he'd said she was family—why not carry the pretence one step farther? Why not pretend she could have Elias forever?

She turned fully sideways in the seat and stared at him openly, her mouth softened with a secret smile. Why had she been afraid to do this before? Why had she let her pride keep her from memorising the features of the man she loved; a memory that would last long beyond the brief limits of their relationship?

'What's wrong?'

Her smile deepened at his question. 'Nothing's wrong.'

The puzzled drop of his brows pulled at her heart, and for the rest of the ride back to Rosewood—back *home*, at least for this one night—Madeline watched his every breath, every movement of his beautiful, long-fingered hands on the wheel, every shadow that passed over the strong, crisp lines of his profile. The sheer freedom of allowing herself to do such a thing intoxicated her.

As if they were ending an awkward first date, Elias unlocked the door, gestured her inside, then hesitated on the step. 'May I come in for a while?'

Her smile was immediate, brilliant. 'It's your house,' she reminded him.

He shook his head. 'No. I promised you that it would be your house, for as long as you stayed.'

'All right, then; it's *our* house,' she replied softly, because that was part of the pretence.

Once inside, Madeline rubbed her arms against the evening chill of the house.

'Cold?' Elias asked.

'A little.'

'It's the dampness. It takes this house a long time to dry out after a rain.'

She turned to him suddenly, child-like anticipation shining in her eyes. 'Would a fire help?'

He arched one dark brow in surprise, then his face softened into a wistful smile. 'I haven't sat in front of a fire for years.'

'I've never sat in front of a fire.'

His eyes held hers for a moment, then without warning he reached out and brushed her cheek with the back of his hand. 'Then tonight you will,' he said gently.

From the very wing chair Elias had sat in earlier, Madeline watched with mute fascination as he laid a fire in the parlour grate. Crouching before the hearth, he was so focused on the placement of logs and kindling that he was unaware of Madeline's gaze. Her grey eyes narrowed as the flames began to lick at the birch logs, lighting him from behind. The outline of his torso beneath his shirt sprang into view, and through a trick of the fickle, wavering light of the fire, his body seemed to shimmer gold beneath the sheer white fabric.

Madeline sat spellbound, memorising the rounded lines of broad shoulders she had never seen before, the ripple of muscles in his back as he lifted another log. She caught her breath, thinking it was like seeing him naked, wondering why she wasn't ashamed to be staring so boldly.

It startled her when he rose suddenly to his feet, brushed his hands against his thighs, then turned to face her. He looked like a god, standing there in the shadows with fire breaking around him, and Madeline found that she couldn't avert her eyes.

She couldn't make out his features with the light behind him, and when he said, 'We need some wine,' it was as if a disembodied spirit had spoken, rather than a flesh-and-blood man.

She took a deep breath when he left the room, and rose to her feet to try to regain her composure. Move, she commanded legs that seemed oddly weak, thinking that the simple act of walking would bring her back down to earth. She paced twice in front of the roaring blaze before she felt the heat caressing her calves beneath the hem of her dress. She stopped suddenly and faced the fire, entranced by the sensation, her lips curved slightly in bemused wonder. Without consciously engineering the act, she sank to her knees and felt the warmth and the light wash over her face.

After a time, she felt a presence and turned to see Elias standing in the doorway, staring at her in quiet wonder. His hands hung forgotten at his sides, a bottle of wine in one, glasses in the other.

I should say something, she thought, filling her eyes with the tousled black crown of his hair, the hard lines of his slender body; but the sight of him seemed to render her speechless. She was helpless to do anything but stare up at him, her lips parted in a moist circle.

'I brought the wine,' he said mindlessly, his voice rumbling across the room and rippling through her body.

She held her breath as he moved slowly towards her, his eyes still locked on hers. She felt the terrified thrill of something grand and powerful approaching, something she would not be able to resist if she allowed it to get too close. Yesterday she would have jumped to her feet and fled, but not tonight. Tonight she was living a dream and in dreams there was no future, no fear of consequences; only the moment.

He towered next to her for a moment and Madeline looked up, awed by the sensations of being a woman shadowed by a man. It was a submissive posture, kneeling at a man's feet like this, and it should have been degrading; but instead there was a strange sense of everything finding its proper place, as if this were exactly where she was supposed to be. He looked down at her, the reflection of yellow flames sparking in the green of his eyes, then sank to his knees facing her, setting wine and glasses aside.

Gently, tenderly, he took her hands and turned her towards him until their knees touched. Dark brows tipped expressively, eyes narrowed in almost painful contemplation, his gaze swept over her face as if he were seeing her for the first—or perhaps the last time.

She was unaware of his hands leaving hers, but they must have, because now his fingers were threading through the silvery lightness of her hair, pushing it away from her face, lifting it from her neck. She shuddered as his hands brushed the tiny hairs at her nape, and her eyes fell closed. 'Elias?' she whispered, and the word was both a question and a plea.

'Say it again,' he murmured hoarsely, and her eyes flew open at what she heard in his voice. 'Say it again, Maddie. Say my name.'

Her heart fluttered in her chest, and for some reason she thought of the old superstition that if you said someone's name, you took possession of their soul—or they took possession of yours; she couldn't remember which. She shook her head wordlessly, suddenly afraid, and he must have seen that in her eyes because he said, 'Don't think about it, Maddie. Don't think about what might happen, or what should happen, or what tomorrow will bring. Think about what we can have now, at this moment, because no other moment exists.'

It was true, she thought, letting her head fall back slightly, shivering at the touch of his hand on her neck. Everything he said was true.

She took his hands in hers and held them as reverently as he had held hers that first night; the beautiful hands that carried poetry from his mind to the music of the keyboard. 'Elias,' she whispered, because that was what he had wanted to hear. 'Elias, Elias, Elias. . .' She repeated it over and over, in time with the beating of her heart, thrilling to the feel and the

sound of it rising from her throat, passing
through her lips, but then suddenly he was
leaning towards her, his hands cradling either
side of her head, his mouth brushing hers to
silence.

'Maddie,' he murmured hoarsely against her
lips, his hands quivering on her upper arms
with passion barely held in check. His jaw
tensed as he pulled her ever so slowly upwards
and against him until their bodies touched from
mouth to knee, as if they were kneeling together
on the altar of desire.

His eyes wandered over her face, touching
each feature in the poignant act of taking possession, and for a moment he said nothing. It
was as if he wanted her to see what his words
would only echo. It was a rare thing, to see
naked emotion on the face of a man; to witness
the awesome passion that made a strong man
suddenly vulnerable.

'From that very first night, Maddie,' he whispered hoarsely. 'This was destined to happen
from that very first night.'

When he kissed her again, every part of her
body strained into his; her face, her hips, her
breasts, filling and growing now with the frantic
pulse of liquid fire, reaching for him, needing
the hard press of his body against hers.

She felt his hands on the back of her neck,
heard the ratchetting sound of her zipper being
pulled down, then heat from the fire on her bare
shoulders as he slipped her dress down to her

waist. He whispered her name over and over again, pulling away, then brushing her mouth with his, then pulling away again. Maddie heard a small, distressed cry of longing leave her lips, and then heard an echo of that cry from his. Finally his arms convulsed, pulling her more tightly against him, and she shuddered as his mouth opened over hers. She gasped when tongue met tongue, and felt herself sag at his answering groan as he lowered her gently on to her back and straddled her on his knees.

Even though they were safely contained within the fireplace, the flames seemed to lick at her bare shoulders and arms, and then suddenly he was opening the front closure of her bra and her breasts felt the lick of his gaze, even hotter than that of the fire, and then the delicate, awed touch of his fingers. He made a sound deep in his throat as he jerked her dress down over her hips and tossed it heedlessly aside.

When he hovered over her, braced by his arms, Madeline reached up and began to fumble at the buttons of his shirt. The graze of her nails against his chest catapulted him to his feet, and he jerked his shirt open, sending buttons flying.

Madeline lay there watching him, clad only in her panties, amazed by her own boldness. Every part of her body throbbed to the beat of an inaudible drum. Her heart stuttered at the sound of his zipper, and she had to concentrate fiercely to keep her eyes locked on his in virginal modesty.

He knelt at her side, carefully removed her panties, then tossed them on to the heap of his own discarded clothing. Madeline glanced over at the untidy pile, struck by the intimacy of their clothing mingling together. She gasped involuntarily as she felt the heat of his bare legs straddling hers, then the great push of air as the rest of his body lowered on to hers.

With his tongue he traced the imaginary lines of a bra beneath her breasts, over the gentle upper swell of the taut mounds, and down into the valley between. She shuddered, then lay still as wisps of his hair trailed behind the path of his mouth. She cried out when his lips finally closed over the quivering, aching peak of her left breast; and when his hand pressed firmly against the flat of her stomach, and then slid downward to part her thighs, she arched her back convulsively upwards, in woman's instinctive welcome to man.

# CHAPTER FOURTEEN

Hours later Madeline drifted upwards from sleep to feel the gentle sweep of a hand across her brow.

'Maddie? Maddie?' a voice whispered, and she rolled to her side and scowled, wanting to sink back into that dream where she and Elias had made love by the fire. . .

Her eyes flew wide open and she found herself staring at the dead ashes in the grate. One by one, her senses came to life. She realised first that she was cold; second, that she was naked.

'It's almost morning, Maddie.' In the faint, sickly light struggling through the windows, she could see him kneeling next to her, dressed already in last night's wrinkled clothes, the buttonless shirt hanging open.

She looked around desperately for something to cover herself because it was all wrong that he should be dressed and she shouldn't, as if his clothing somehow mocked her nudity. It wasn't the way she'd dreamed she would wake up after her first night of love. He was supposed to be cradling her in his arms, murmuring the unimaginable things lovers must say to each other in the morning.

She jerked to a sitting position, hugged herself and rubbed briskly at the goose-flesh on her arms. Elias grabbed an afghan from a nearby chair and wrapped it around her shoulders, but the gesture seemed more hurried than solicitous.

'We have to hurry, Maddie. We'll have to leave soon to get to the city on time.' He smiled and chucked her under the chin, as if she were a child he was cajoling out of bed.

Her grey eyes warmed to a near-charcoal colour, she reached over with one finger and touched the corner of his mouth. The memory of what that mouth had done to her last night made her blush furiously. 'We fell asleep,' she mumbled, still groggy. She smiled as her gaze wandered over the dark morning stubble peppering his strong jaw, the tumble of black hair falling over his brow.

'We did indeed.' He stroked the long tangles of her light hair back from her face, and she shivered under his touch as the afghan slipped from her shoulders to puddle at her waist. She felt her nipples pucker in the cold, and, astonished by her own boldness, she took Elias's hand and pressed it against the swelling firmness of her breast.

'God, Maddie,' he hissed between his teeth, his eyes narrowing, the black pupil expanding to nearly obscure the green; but then suddenly his face tightened and a line of urgency appeared between his brows. 'We can't do this,' he whispered hoarsely. 'We have to hurry.' He flashed a brief, hard smile, then rose to his feet and looked down at her. 'Becky will be here any minute. We certainly don't want her walking in on this, do we?'

Madeline's smile faltered and it seemed that the floor shifted beneath her as the reality of morning pushed last night's fantasy aside. Last night there had been no music, no past, no future—and no Becky—but last night was over. She felt an icy chill that had nothing to do with the temperature of the room, and scrambled to her feet, clutching the afghan around her.

She looked up at the beautiful, chiselled face; the green eyes quiet and disturbingly innocent, as if he hadn't just betrayed one woman and used another. It seemed impossible that the mind behind such a face, the mind that created such beauty in music, could ever be capable of treachery, and yet obviously it was. And Madeline had been his partner.

With all her strength of will she tried to hate him, yet he still had the power to tug at her heart, to twist it in his hands; and so because she couldn't hate him, she ended up hating herself instead.

When he reached for her shoulder she scrambled backwards, her face contorted with the effort of holding back the tears.

Startled, Elias reached for her again, then jerked back when she cried out, 'No! Don't touch me!'

He froze in place and whispered, 'My God, Maddie. What's wrong?'

She bit down on her lip, swallowing the traitorous sob that rose from her throat. 'It should never have happened—last night should never have happened. . .you had no right. . .' Her voice cracked and the dam that had been holding her emotions back for years crumbled, releasing the flood of her tears.

Elias's expression stilled with shock. 'Maddie, Maddie. . . I'm sorry. I thought you wanted it, too. . . I didn't mean to hurt you. . .' His eyes darted over her face as if they couldn't believe what they saw through the pain. 'Dear God,' he whispered, his lips barely moving. He looked down, touching a hand briefly to his creased brow, and when he looked up again, his eyes were empty as if all the feeling had been drained from him.

Without another word, he turned and walked away.

Madeline stood under the hot spray of the shower longer than she should have, trying to steam away the tears and the emotions that prompted them—emotions that threatened to overwhelm her.

You can handle this, Madeline, she told herself, scrubbing at her skin until it flamed red, thinking that maybe if she hurt enough on the outside, the pain on the inside wouldn't seem so bad.

The prospect of riding to the city in the same car as Elias and Becky horrified her, but there was no time to make other arrangements.

She towelled dry quickly, combed out her wet hair, then dressed in the floor-length black jersey dress she wore for student recitals. She gazed indifferently at her reflection as she put on a minimum of make-up, remembering that the high-necked black dress always made her look as though she was in mourning. Today that seemed very appropriate.

The ride to the city was every bit as nightmarish as she had imagined it would be. At her own insistence she sat in the back seat, curled in a corner pretending to sleep, while Becky talked to Elias about everything from village gossip to the musical talent of a young boy they both knew.

Elias was sullen and withdrawn at first, but eventually Becky's conversational prodding seemed to make him relax. Once it made him chuckle, and the sound tore at the fabric of Madeline's heart. By the time they had reached the city, she had a headache from squeezing her eyes shut, trying to block out the sounds from the front seat.

'We're here.' Elias parked in the dimness of a city parking ramp, shut off the engine, and turned in the seat to look at her. 'Are you awake?'

'Just about.' She pretended a yawn that quickly became real.

'Well, come on, then.'

Madeline lagged behind the twosome, noticing almost against her will the way Elias looked at Becky, and who could blame him? She was even more beautiful today than usual, if such a thing were possible. She'd worn a smart black suit perfectly tailored to her voluptuous curves, with a skirt short enough to reveal the shapely calves that scissored beneath it. Those snapping, hot eyes of hers were even more dramatic with make-up, and her hair looked like a dark waterfall that sparked with fiery highlights every time she swung her head.

Even if they'd been three friends with nothing to hide from each other, Madeline would have walked in their shadow. Being close to Becky made her feel uglier than ever.

The album cover was to be photographed at the very concert hall where Madeline had first played for Elias, and there was a bitter irony to that. As they approached from the wings, Elias and Becky dropped back, and it was Madeline who first recoiled from the chaotic scene that sullied the normally pristine stage. Even the imposing concert grand seemed lost in the clutter of lights and cameras and hurrying, shouting people.

Suddenly a figure rushed towards her from the confusion, arms outstretched, and Madeline almost wept at the comforting sight of that brilliant, familiar smile.

'Angel!' David cried a greeting, and Madeline

surprised herself by digging deep enough to find a smile of her own.

Look at him, she thought as he approached, the sight of his dark, unruly curls and the merry sparkle of his eyes somehow comforting her. Could it be so hard to love this particular man? After all, Elias said that David was in love with her; surely she could learn, in time, to return the feeling. . .but then she glanced back at Elias, at the crisp, ascetic line of his profile, the black slash of his swept-back hair, and realised she could never love another man. . .not while Elias Shepherd lived in the same world.

'Hello, David.' She smiled with genuine affection, more grateful than he would ever know for the gift of his love, even if she couldn't return it. Her smile faltered when he folded her into an embrace, because somehow it was different from the way he'd held her at Rosewood. It seemed a little stiff, almost distant, as if he, too, were pulling away from her. In the next moment, she realised why.

'David?' Becky's voice came from just behind her, and Madeline watched David's face as he looked over her shoulder. The sparkle in his brown eyes seemed to melt with the unmistakable warmth of love, and his smile softened.

Madeline watched in amazement as he stepped quickly around her, then swept Becky into an embrace she suspected didn't feel distant at all. She'd seen it in his eyes, and now she saw it in the tender, reverent touch of his hand on Becky's cheek.

In that moment Madeline felt the fires of resentment flame high within her, and she had to bite down on the impulse to cry out against the unfairness of life. It was so simple for Becky—not only did she command the adoration of the man Madeline loved, but of the only man who might have loved Madeline.

She stood in numb disbelief as David guided Becky and Elias on-stage before the camera, then scurried off to the other side.

Time had no meaning for Madeline as the photographer shouted instructions, adjusted and readjusted lights, shot picture after picture of Becky sitting at the piano with Elias behind her. She saw everything that happened, but it was as if she were seeing it through a veil; removing herself to a distant place where pain could not reach her. She came to full attention only when the photographer finally shouted in frustration, 'Dammit, I can't get it. It's just not there. Have that girl play the music; maybe that'll get them into the mood, and then we'll try again.'

Madeline sighed and moved woodenly across the stage to sit at the piano. She stared down vacantly, as if she'd never seen a keyboard before.

'Play "Heartsong", Maddie,' Elias's voice came from somewhere behind her. 'Heartsong'—so that was what he'd named the theme song for the movie. Her hands lifted automatically and she wondered if she would always obey that voice, no matter what it asked, and then her left hand came down on the keys in a powerful bass chord that seemed to cry from the depths of a tortured man's soul. Every voice in the hall immediately fell silent.

The first part of the overture was dark and full of thundering pathos, mirroring Madeline's own despair—exactly the kind of music that had first drawn her to Elias's compositions, with one exception. Unlike the ponderous, brooding scores the critics had panned, there was a counterpoint in this piece—a trembling treble dance that rose lightly, delicately over the pounding bass chords like the hopeful promise of spring after a late winter storm.

Transported by the music, Madeline bent earnestly over the piano, her long, pale hair shimmering like a fall of crystal beneath the bright lights. In this, if in nothing else—as long as the music he wrote found its voice through her hands—she and Elias were irrevocably joined.

Her concentration was so great that she never noticed the rapt attention of everyone in the hall, the sense of so many holding a collective breath, waiting, waiting for something. . .nor did she wonder whose hand it was, suddenly pressing lightly against her shoulder. But then the music began to rise, lifting in a dance of

melodic brilliance that fulfilled its earlier promise, and she knew it was Elias's hand on her
shoulder. Once again she felt the current of his
spirit flowing from his hand through her body
to the keyboard, making her his instrument just
as the piano was hers.

The feeling was so intense that a shudder
passed through her, but she knew that feeling
would last only as long as this particular
performance.

Let it happen, she told herself, filling the air
with the musical flight of her fantasy. Pretend
for this one last time that the music is only the
sound of the two of you loving each other.

It was easy, then, to close her eyes and let her
heart rise with the sounds of joy her fingers
were making. It was easy to pretend that the
fingers on her shoulder were pressing harder
into her flesh, lending her his power, somehow
joining his spirit with hers and taking them both
higher than they had ever been before.

Behind her closed eyes she saw stars going
nova, the dazzling explosion of fireworks
against a night sky, and her heart and her hands
and the music rode up to greet them. Somewhere beyond the song, as if from a great
distance, she heard someone shouting, 'That's
it! That's perfect! Don't stop!' but the voice
seemed part of a dream that only ended when
her hands struck the final, triumphant chord.

And then there was silence.

Madeline slumped on the bench, her eyes still

closed, feeling that at last she had given everything she had to give, and now she was empty.

She was vaguely aware of low murmurs
finally breaking the silence, gradually increasing
in volume until it seemed that everyone around
her was shouting with excitement—everyone
but Elias. He was still behind her; she could feel
his presence like the heat of the sun on her back;
but he said nothing.

She looked up at the sound of feet pounding
across the wooden stage, and saw the photographer racing towards them, David and Backy and
other people she didn't know close behind.
Their faces all looked so strange, she thought;
caught in that odd, tight expression that lay
halfway between laughter and tears.

'For God's sake, why didn't the two of you
pose together in the first place?' the photographer demanded breathlessly.

Madeline blinked at him, baffled by the question. Behind her, she heard Elias clear his throat
nervously.

'I'm telling you,' the photographer babbled
on, 'I got more shots of the two of you in sixty
seconds than I got in that whole first hour. . .'
He turned quickly to Becky, apologising. 'No
offence to you, miss. You're about as pretty as
they come, but. . .'

Amazingly, Becky grinned at him. 'You don't
have to apologise to me. I saw what——'

'What do you mean, you got shots of us?'
Madeline interrupted.

'The pictures, angel.' David moved to sit next to her and took her hand. 'Didn't you see the flashbulbs going off?'

Madeline shook her head wordlessly, wondering how she could have missed anything as vivid as flashbulbs—and then her expression cleared as she remembered the stars going nova; the fireworks she'd seen behind closed eyes.

'Now, I know you weren't too keen on the idea of posing for the album cover,' David was saying, 'but there wasn't a person in this room who didn't see on this stage exactly what should be on that album. . .you and Elias. Together.'

The photographer chuckled. 'You can't fool the camera, you know. You want a picture of two people in love? Take a picture of two people in love!'

Madeline stiffened on the bench, her hand going suddenly cold in David's. Dear lord, had she been so transparent? Could everyone see how she felt about Elias, merely by looking at her face? 'No,' she said quickly, wanting desperately to deny it before Elias did. 'That's not what you saw. We love the music, not each other.'

Becky knew she was lying; Madeline could see it in her face. The beautiful brown eyes snapped with icy hatred that seemed to be a warning.

Don't worry, Becky, Madeline thought with a rueful smile. I may love Elias, but you'll get no competition from me. You're the woman he loves.

Suddenly Becky's eyes jerked to look behind Madeline, widened with something like alarm, then narrowed when they shifted back to her again. 'Nice work, Madeline,' she spat viciously, then she pushed her way around the bench and disappeared.

Madeline sighed and closed her eyes, trying to slip down into that place deep inside where pain didn't reach, but David wouldn't let her. He was still next to her on the bench, and now his arm was around her shoulders and he was whispering into her ear. 'You're killing him, angel. Can't you see that?'

She frowned hard, wondering why nothing anyone said today made any sense. If only they would all leave her alone; if only she could just disappear. . .

She heard Becky call to David from somewhere off-stage, smiled sadly at how quickly he jumped to answer the call, then watched in indifference as the others drifted away from the piano one by one. Show's over, folks, she thought bitterly.

She didn't know how long she had been sitting there alone when Becky appeared suddenly at her side, her face set in a rigid mask of fury.

'All right, come on,' she snapped, jerking her thumb towards the door. 'Thanks to you, we'll have to drive ourselves home in David's car. Eli left without us.'

Madeline frowned at yet another development that didn't make sense at all. Elias might have been embarrassed by what the photographer had said; perhaps even angry that such a thing had been said in front of Becky; but that wasn't much of a reason to storm off and leave them both behind.

As it turned out, it wasn't. The real reason was worse.

'Why would he leave us stranded?' she asked Becky in a small voice.

'Because he can't bear to be with you,' Becky said coldly. 'That's why. Not let's go.'

Madeline nodded absently, shrugging into that old cloak of indifference that had protected her for so many years.

# CHAPTER FIFTEEN

MADELINE sat rigidly in the passenger seat as Becky drove David's car towards Rosewood in furious, tight-lipped silence. What does *she* have to be angry about? Madeline thought, bitterness pricking through the numbness she felt. At last she's getting everything she wanted—Elias back at Rosewood, me out of the way. . .

Her thoughts paused, as if to give her time to examine them. She hadn't realised until that moment that she had finally surrendered to the inevitable; she was ready to leave Rosewood.

She sighed and turned her head to watch the countryside race past her window, thinking of the first time Elias had driven her to Rosewood. Had it really been less than a month ago? The world had seemed as bright as her future that day, with spring exploding everywhere she'd looked. This afternoon low-hanging clouds rested fat, dark bellies on the horizon, and Madeline seemed to feel their weight on her shoulders.

'How will David get his car back?' she asked at last, not really caring, just weary of the strained silence.

Becky's mouth twitched irritably. 'I'll take it

back in tonight. I was supposed to stay in and have dinner with him anyway.'

Madeline turned to look at her, pale brows arched slightly. 'You were going to have dinner with David?'

'Yes-I-was-going-to-have-dinner-with-David,' Becky parroted sarcastically. 'What of it?'

'Well. . .doesn't Elias mind?'

'Why should he?'

'Why should he?' Madeline echoed weakly. 'How can you ask that? He even *told* David you were off limits, the day they went to your house to talk about the album cover. . .'

Becky's mouth tightened with impatience. 'No wonder David was so nervous that day,' she mumbled, more to herself than to Madeline. 'I should have guessed Elias had said something like that.'

'He should have married you in the first place,' Madeline muttered, looking down at where her hands twined together in her lap.

'Wha-at?' Becky almost shouted, and the car swerved as her hands jerked convulsively on the wheel. 'Good God, Madeline! What an awful thing to say!'

Madeline blinked at her, bewildered. 'Why? What's so awful about it?'

'What's so awful about it?' Becky demanded. 'Are you out of your mind? Marry my own *brother*?'

Becky was still talking—ranting, really, if the look on her face was any indication—but

Madeline could no longer hear her. For a moment she heard nothing but the frantic scrambling of her own thoughts, trying to make sense of a world suddenly turned upside down.

'Your brother?' she finally managed to whisper. 'Elias. . .is. . .your. . .*brother*?'

Very slowly, Becky turned her head to look at her, dark brows tipped suspiciously. 'Of course he's my brother,' she said carefully. 'Well, half-brother, actually—you knew that. . .' When she saw Madeline's wide eyes, her head shaking back and forth in mute astonishment, the suspicion in her face was replaced by angry disbelief. 'How could you not know that?' she asked, glaring at the road ahead as if there were great sin in Madeline's ignorance.

'No one told me,' Madeline whispered, barely moving her lips.

'But you knew who I was when I came to the house that first day,' Becky insisted, scowling. 'You said Elias told you I was coming. . .'

'He said you were coming; that you'd drive out from the village every day to cook and clean. . .he didn't say you were his sister——'

'Half-sister,' Becky corrected automatically. 'We had the same father—different mothers.'

Madeline sat motionless, trying to remember to blink, to breathe. 'You didn't grow up together?' she whispered.

Becky shook her head. 'After Elias's parents were divorced, Dad married my mother and they had me. We lived further upstate and I never even met Elias until he and his mom came to the funeral. . .' Her voice began to crack and she had to pause a moment to collect herself. 'I'd just finished college when my folks were killed in a car accident—my whole family gone in the blink of an eye—or so I thought. At the funeral Elias and his mother told me I had family in Brighton Square, and it was time I got to know them—can you imagine that? I moved there a year later, and until the day she died I loved Elias's mother almost as much as I'd loved my own.'

Madeline sat in stunned silence, seeing the shadow of Elias in Becky's profile for the first time. Her mind stumbled through all the things that had happened at Rosewood, trying to make sense of them.

'So that's the story,' Becky was saying, 'although I can't imagine what difference it makes.'

Madeline stared straight ahead, barely blinking, her hands limp in her lap. 'All this time,' she murmured, her voice barely audible over the noise of the engine. 'All this time I thought you were lovers.'

Becky's face froze. 'What?' she whispered.

Madeline nodded woodenly. 'The way he talked about you, the way you acted when you were together. . .so many little things. . .it was obvious there was a special relationship between you, and I just thought it was. . .'

'Oh, my God,' Becky groaned.

'And you hated me,' Madeline added under her breath. 'The more I loved Elias, the more you hated me. . .'

Becky's hair flew as she spun her head to look at her. 'You love Elias?' she whispered.

Madeline nodded, her lower lip quivering.

Becky stared at the road for a long moment, her head shaking almost imperceptibly. 'Madeline,' she finally said without looking at her, 'I hated you because I thought you *didn't* love him. He called me the night he met you, told me to hurry over to the house and clean the bedroom, because he was bringing home the woman he wanted to marry; the woman who'd given him back his music. . .'

Madeline caught her breath and stared at her. 'He never told me that. He never said a thing. . .'

Becky made a face. 'Of course he didn't. You were his pianist, just like his wife. . .it was all too much like what happened the first time, and that terrified him.'

Madeline remembered that first day in the studio, when Elias had been so desperate to keep emotional involvement from interfering with the music. . .

'But he couldn't help himself,' Becky went on. 'It was impossible for him to think of you as just a friend. . .as you know very well from what happened last night.'

Madeline's head flew sideways to look at her. 'You *know* what happened last night?'

Becky's expression tightened. 'Only what he told me—that he finally gave in to what he'd felt from the beginning; that he finally risked everything. . .and this morning you threw it all back in his face.'

'I thought he loved you,' Madeline whispered. 'I thought it had all been a terrible mistake. . .' Her words faded as she faced front and stared through the windscreen, realising that the mistakes had started long before last night, long before she and Elias had even met each other.

She smiled sadly, thinking that the baggage they'd both carried into this relationship had nearly destroyed it. Just because no one had ever loved her, she thought no one ever could; and just because Elias had been betrayed once, he thought love itself had betrayed him—that his impulse to love could never be trusted again. They had been so busy following the lessons of the past, listening to the warnings of memory, that they had almost lost their chance for the future.

So many mistakes, she mused, watching the ribbon of tar slip beneath the car; so many misunderstandings, right from the beginning, and it had all happened because they'd ignored what the music was telling them; they'd forgotten that music was nothing more than a song that comes from the heart.

Suddenly Madeline straightened in the seat, eyes fastened to the road ahead, every muscle in her body tensed. 'Hurry, Becky,' she whispered. 'I have to see Elias. I have to get home.'

Becky smiled a little, then pressed harder on the accelerator and gave her full attention to the road.

# CHAPTER SIXTEEN

AFTER Becky had dropped her off, Madeline stood for a moment in the front garden looking at the house—at the brilliant white of the newly painted shutters, the neatly tended shrubbery around the front door—the changes she'd made to tell the world that she had been there. She smiled at the lily of the valley she'd uncovered yesterday, bobbing now in the cool shade beneath the shrubs, as if ringing their little white bells in welcome. Behind her the dark bellies of low-scudding clouds kissed the horizon in their distant race eastward, while overhead only a thin layer of white remained to obscure the sun.

'Elias?' she called out as she entered the house. She closed the door behind her and stood in the quiet foyer, listening to the echo of her own voice. The silence should have been empty, yet to Madeline it seemed full of promise. There was the steady, distant tick of the clock in the kitchen; the murmuring hum of the refrigerator—all the sounds of a house not abandoned, but simply waiting to welcome its owners home.

On her way back to the kitchen the hem of her black jersey dress brushed the wooden floor like a caress. Head high, an almost ethereal smile gracing her lips, she trailed one hand

along the wall as she passed, taking possession.
Mine, she thought, cherishing the word, the
concept of belonging. This house can be mine;
Elias can be mine; everything I've ever wanted
can be mine—all I have to do is reach out and
take it.

She hesitated at the kitchen door, wondering
if home and love and family had always been
within her reach. She had never protested her
fate; never felt worthy enough of love to ask for
it openly; maybe that was part of the reason
family after family had sent that cold little girl
away—because she'd never let them see all the
love in her heart.

She felt the weight of the past lift suddenly
and simply drift away. Her feet barely touched
the floor as she walked to the kitchen window
and looked outside.

Elias was out there, kneeling in her rose
garden, still dressed in the tuxedo he'd worn to
the city. She saw his bent head through the
glass as he worked at the base of a plant, his
black hair quivering with the motion of his
hands.

As she went outside to join him, she didn't
feel like a woman merely walking towards the
man she loved; she felt like a warm, frothy wave
being pulled inexorably from the black sea
towards the bright shore of its destiny.

She stopped next to him and looked down at
the empty green eyes looking up. 'You're a little
overdressed for this kind of work,' she said.

'We're going to have to get you some gardening clothes.'

His black brows twitched in a puzzled frown, and Madeline felt an aching flood of tenderness wash over her.

He glanced down at the soil-encrusted knees of the black trousers and shrugged indifferently. When he looked up at her again, he flinched slightly, and she wondered if the change within her was clearly visible on her face. For just an instant the protective curtain lifted from his eyes, and Madeline glimpsed hope, longing, pain—the reflection of all her own old emotions—and then the curtain crashed down and his face grew cold.

'I won't have much use for gardening clothes. I don't intend to stay at Rosewood.'

It was such a strange sensation, to smile at words that would have sent her spirits plummeting just a short time ago. It didn't matter if they left Rosewood, because now she knew that the home she'd longed for wasn't a place—even a place she loved as much as this one.

'All right,' she said quietly. 'If you want us to go somewhere else, we will.'

He looked up at her, his face expressionless. 'What are you talking about? You should know better than anyone we can't work together any more. It's just too. . .hard.'

'Why?' she asked, trying to keep her voice light. Inside her head she was screaming at him to say it, to just say it out loud, once and for all;

that if Becky was right and he'd really loved her all this time, why couldn't he just say it?

'You know perfectly well why,' he mumbled at the ground.

'Tell me. I want to hear you say it out loud,' she insisted, her voice trembling. Her hands were clenched at her sides and her whole body was leaning forward, her future hanging on his response.

'Dammit!' He flung a handful of soil down at the ground and jumped to his feet. 'You want to hear it out loud? All right! Becase I can't keep that damn agreement! I can't go on pretending that all I feel for you is friendship. . .' Suddenly he closed his eyes and his shoulders sagged. 'Love keeps getting in the way,' he said quietly. 'I already told you all this—that morning David was at the house, remember?'

Madeline's face reflected an instant of pain. She remembered that morning; remembered Elias telling her that emotions had interfered with their working relationship from the beginning—but she'd thought he'd been talking about *her* emotions, not his.

'You love me,' she murmured, awestruck by the sound of the words.

His mouth twisted in a self-deprecating smile and he looked off to one side. 'That's been pretty obvious right from the start, hasn't it?' he asked drily. 'And it was more than you bargained for. *That* was pretty obvious, too. So now it's all out in the open; the pretending is over. Are you satisfied now?' He spun his head to glare at her, then winced to see her smiling at his pain. 'I think you should go pack your things, Maddie,' he said tonelessly, looking away again. 'I'll drive you home.'

There was a brief moment of stabbing uncertainty, of faltering courage, as Madeline remembered all the other times in her life people had told her she had to leave. . .

She closed her eyes briefly, then clenched her jaw with determination. Not this time. 'I *am* home,' she said quietly, and he turned his head slowly to look at her. His face—that strong, beautiful, beloved face—slipped in and out of focus as her eyes filled with tears. 'I knew I was home the first time I saw your face,' she added in a whisper. 'I just didn't think you wanted me.'

His mouth sagged open and the words came out in a whispered gasp. 'You didn't think *I* wanted *you*?'

Her lips quivered as she nodded and blinked, watching his eyes darken with the look of one afraid to embrace joy, for fear it would be snatched away. It was a look she knew well— she'd seen it in the mirror a thousand times. There were so many things she had to tell him, so many things that needed explaining, but now was not the time.

She smiled at him through her tears, marvelling at how very much alike they had always been—both so wounded by rejection that they had learned to fear love itself; both so blinded by that fear that they couldn't see love in the other one's eyes.

'Maddie?' he whispered once, his eyes searching her face, then shining with the green of spring's promise after a lifetime of winter. 'You love me,' he murmured, his voice as filled with wonder as hers had been when she'd said the very same words. 'My God, you love me. . .'

Suddenly he grabbed her by the shoulders, his eyes narrowed, his voice a low rasp. 'Say it,' he demanded. 'Tell me you love me, Madeline. Say it aloud.'

Her lips moved, struggling to find the shape of the words she'd never said, but before she could speak his mouth was busy on her face, his hands were threading into her hair and she could barely catch her breath at all, let alone speak.

'Say it!' he hissed close to her ear, and she felt the words she had never spoken in her life fly from her mouth as he jerked her against him.

It didn't even feel strange, telling Elias she loved him. After all, she'd been telling him that ever since they met, the only way she knew how, whenever she played his music.

She didn't question the power of the force that brought them both to their knees; she never felt the damp soil cushion her head or the thorny caress of a rose bush against her hand as she reached out to pull love against her—she knew only that together she and Elias were celebrating life, embracing it as surely as they embraced each other.

Once, for just a moment, her eyes fluttered open. Above her Elias's face was framed by the tattered veil of clouds that had finally been shredded by the wind. Through the white lace, the light and the warmth that was life itself shone down, and, next to where Elias and Madeline lay, the first rosebud lifted its face for the kiss of the sun.

HARLEQUIN ◆ PRESENTS®

# BARBARY WHARF

### Home to the *Sentinel*
### Home to passion, heartache and love

*Charlotte Lamb*

The BARBARY WHARF six-book saga continues with Book Three, TOO CLOSE FOR COMFORT. Esteban Sebastian is the *Sentinel*'s marketing director *and* the company heartthrob. But beautiful Irena Olivero wants nothing to do with him—he's always too close for comfort.

And don't forget media tycoon Nick Caspian and his adversary Gina Tyrrell. Their never-ending arguments are legendary—but is it possible that things are not quite what they seem?

TOO CLOSE FOR COMFORT (Harlequin Presents #1513) available in December.

HARLEQUIN PRESENTS®

## *A Year Down Under*

Beginning in January 1993, some of Harlequin
Presents's most exciting authors will join us as we
celebrate the land down under by featuring one title
per month set in Australia or New Zealand.

Intense, passionate romances, these stories will take
you from the heart of the Australian outback to the
wilds of New Zealand, from the sprawling cattle and
sheep stations to the sophistication of cities like
Sydney and Auckland.

Share the adventure—and the romance—
of A Year Down Under!

Don't miss our first visit in
HEART OF THE OUTBACK by Emma Darcy,
Harlequin Presents #1519, available in January
wherever Harlequin Books are sold.     YDU-G

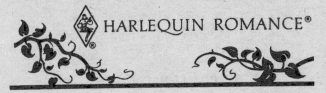

# HARLEQUIN ROMANCE®

After her father's heart attack, Stephanie Bloomfield comes home to Orchard Valley, Oregon, to be with him and with her sisters.

*Orchard Valley*

Steffie learns that many things have changed in her absence—but not her feelings for journalist Charles Tomaselli. He was the reason she left Orchard Valley. Now, three years later, will he give her a reason to stay?

"The Orchard Valley trilogy features three delightful, spirited sisters and a trio of equally fascinating men. The stories are rich with the romance, warmth of heart and humor readers expect, and invariably receive, from Debbie Macomber."

—Linda Lael Miller

Don't miss the Orchard Valley trilogy by Debbie Macomber:

VALERIE   Harlequin Romance #3232 (November 1992)
STEPHANIE   Harlequin Romance #3239 (December 1992)
NORAH   Harlequin Romance #3244 (January 1993)

Look for the special cover flash on each book!

Available wherever Harlequin books are sold.   ORC-2